The Bully

TOM PUMA

Fulton Books
Meadville, PA

Published by Fulton Books 2023

ISBN 979-8-88731-122-7 (paperback)
ISBN 979-8-88731-123-4 (digital)

Printed in the United States of America

To my friend Billy Sutter and his wife, Rose.
To Melody, Jackie, and Susan, and all those who
have been bullied and fought back.

On July 1, 2020, the construction crew was ready to start the remodel of expanding the boiler room at a high school in Upstate New York. All the old boilers were being removed and replaced by larger, more efficient ones. The foreman, Steve Johnson, was checking out a wall that would have to come down for the expansion. It was a cinder block wall eight feet high and eight feet wide. The demolition men were standing by, awaiting orders to start with sledgehammers and chains to pull the wall down. It was a dimly lit room with old incandescing bulbs that hadn't been changed to LED lights. Steve thought of the best way to bring the wall down without making too much of a mess. He then realized, being blocked, he could cut out a section with chop saws and pull it down from the top, using the chains and a few good strong bodies.

"Charlie, go get a chop saw with a good wide masonry blade. We're going to pull this wall down in one shot," he ordered.

Soon Charlie came back with the chop saw, and they were cutting a vertical line up the wall in two-foot sections. After about thirty minutes, the first section was ready to come down.

"Okay, let's drill two holes in the top there and get our toggles in and hook the chains up," said Steve.

A man put a ladder in place, then climbed up and started drilling two three-inch holes, which he completed in ten minutes. He then placed two large toggle bolts through the hole, which expanded on the other side. The front of the toggle had a loop to attach a chain. After all this was done, four big men came over, and as two grabbed one chain, the other two grabbed the other chain Steve gave the order to pull. The four men started to back up, pulling hard.

"She's breaking loose, guys, keep pulling. It's coming, keep pulling," Steve yelled.

The men gave one big yank on the chain, and the top of the wall broke free, and soon the whole section came down with a crash, and a cloud of dust filled the room. There was choking and coughing as everyone waited for the dust to clear.

"Is everyone okay?" asked Steve.

"Everyone, just stay put till this dust clears up," said the foreman.

When the dust finally cleared, all the men moved toward the opening. All jaws dropped, and eyes fixed on a sight that they could not imagine in their wildest nightmare. There seated in an old school chair, was a body. It was tied up, gagged with duct tape, and the chair was tied to a rebar so the person could not reach the wall to try and knock it down. They all just stood petrified. No one had ever seen anything so gruesome in their lives.

"Call 911, quick. We can't go any further. Tell the crew to go home. No one else comes in here. You understand, Charlie?"

"Got it, boss. Come on, guys, let's get out of here. We're all going to have nightmares tonight."

As they all exited the boiler room, Charlie got on the phone.

"Hello, 911? You need to send some cops to High School 41. We got a body. Looks like it's been there for over fifty years. Yeah. My foreman will be waiting down there."

As Charlie spoke to the police, the other men told the crew what they found. There was a commotion among the men.

"Okay, guys, we can't go any further. I guess you know we found a body down there. Steve says for everyone to go home today. This place is a crime scene now. The cops will be here soon and probably put up police tape around this whole area," said Charlie.

The men all started to put the gear away back in the storage container and headed for their cars. Charlie stood outside and waited for the police to arrive. He nearly got through half of his cigarette when he heard sirens coming from down the street. As two squad cars and one unmarked car drove up the driveway to the school, they all pulled up right where Charlie stood.

An officer got out of each squad car then two detectives got out of the unmarked vehicle. One was an elderly man in his mid-fifties, white with salt and pepper hair, a small mustache, a loose tie, and a suit that looked like it hadn't been dry cleaned in months. The other was a younger white woman, very neat in appearance, and hair put back like she just got out of the military. Walking up to Charlie, each reached for their badges.

"My name is Sergeant Gerald Higgins, this is Detective Jackie Summers. What do we have here?"

"You better go down to the boiler room and see for yourselves. You'll find my foreman Steve Johnson down there waiting for you. Just go right down that staircase over there, Detectives."

"Let's go, Jackie, back to school," said Higgins.

They walked over to the staircase leading to the boiler room. Higgins turned to the other officers.

"You two stay up here, make sure nobody comes down here."

They could smell the smoke from Steve's cigarette as they came into the boiler room. Steve turned to see them enter.

"Are you the foreman here running this job?" asked Higgins.

"Yes, sir, I am. Steve Johnson." He reached to shake hands.

"I'm Detective Higgins, and this is Detective Summers. Where is it?"

"Right over here, Detective."

Steve led them to the wall they had just taken down. Both detectives froze in their tracks when they saw the sight. Jackie put her hands to her mouth.

"Oh my god."

"That's pretty much what my men said when they saw it," replied Steve.

Higgins turned to Jackie.

"Boy, this is a new one. I've seen a lot of murders in my life, but never anything like this. Better get the medical examiner here, he's going to have a time with this one."

Higgins stepped inside the wall to get a closer look. He eyed the clothing on the body. The shoes and the way they had been tied up. Then he noticed something interesting in the pocket of the jacket, the corner of a piece of paper. He very gently opened the jacket, pulled out a paper, unfolded it, and began to read.

"Clyde Butcher (Bully). But he will bully no more. He got what was coming to him."

"Well, I guess we know who our victim was now," said Higgins, holding up the note. "His name was Clyde Butcher. I guess he was the bully of the school here, and someone just had enough of his shit. And judging from the clothes he's wearing, I make it out to be around the late sixties. This guy has been here for a long time."

There came a voice from outside.

"Medical examiner is here."

"Okay, send him down," replied Jackie.

"Until we figure this out, you and your men will have to stay clear of this place," said Higgins.

"I understand, Detective. We have other jobs we can do. This one will have to wait. Do you need anything further from me?" replied Steve.

"No, you can go if you want."

As Steve walked off, the two detectives looked at the body.

"Boy, what a way to get even with a bully. I mean, I had bullies at school, but I would never think of anything like this. This guy must have been a real piece of work," said Jackie.

"Yeah, I had them too, but usually, when you stand up to them, they back down. At least that's what the bullies in my school did. I guess this guy just didn't want to give in, and someone decided to stop him, permanently," replied Higgins.

"Where do you want to start, Higgins?" asked Jackie.

"Well, I guess we should start by checking out old yearbooks, old teachers if they are still alive, and old schoolmates, see if anyone can remember this guy. We know his name, so it shouldn't be too hard to find out when he went to school here and who he hung out with if he even had any friends."

"I wonder if his parents are still around?" asked Jackie.

"Good point, we should probably check there first," replied Higgins.

Just then, there came a voice from behind.

"Hey, Gerald, you call for the medical examiner?"

"Hey, Pete, nice to see you again. Jackie, this is Pete Fargo. We both started around the same time working for the bureau. If there's anyone who knows his way around a body, it's this guy."

"Nice to meet you Pete," replied Jackie.

Pete walked over to where the body was.

"Wow, what do we have here. Silence of the Lambs? Looks like the sixties to me from his clothes."

"That's what we gathered too, Pete," said Higgins. "He had this stuffed in his pocket."

Pete took the note and read it.

"Boy, Karma sure is a bitch."

"I'll say. Never liked bullies. Still don't. Well, I'll leave you to it, Pete. We are going to have a look around here, see if we can pick up any other evidence. Come on, Jackie, let's go get ahold of the principal of this place. Time to get some answers," said Higgins.

"I'm with you, boss."

Both started up the stairs and headed for their cars. Looking around, they noticed a little crowd started forming on the sidewalk nearby. Many of them had children who attended this school. Some of the men standing there with their wives were asking questions to the police blocking the entrance, but no answers were given. Just then, all saw the gurney come out with a body bag, then they all knew someone had died there. But who? After watching them put the body in the vehicle, one squad car stayed behind while they took the body away. Higgins and Jackie headed back to the office to figure out their first step: who, what, when, where, and why. As they drove back to the office, Jackie turned to Higgins.

"You know, I just can't get over how that body was never discovered until now. Didn't anyone smell an odor from the decay? We're talking fifty years here."

"Well, let's get back to the office. I'll try working on some old teachers if they are still alive. You try looking up any old schoolmates," replied Higgins.

"What about the parents?" said Jackie.

Higgins gave Jackie the thumbs up and said, "You're learning, Summers, you're learning." Jackie gave a slight smile of pride.

Back at the school, people were gathered outside watching the whole event with police cars and squad car lights flickering all around the schoolyard. Across the street, there was one house where the window blinds were just barely opened. Two eyes peered through, then suddenly shut.

One of the police officers walked over to the crowd and said, "Okay, folks, there isn't too much left to see here, we need to clear this area."

"What happened, officer? We saw them take a body out," said a woman standing by.

"Seems the workers found a body hidden behind a wall in the boiler room. Some kid named Clyde. He was some kind of bully back years ago. I guess someone got a little fed up with his bullying and decided enough is enough. They found him tied to a chair and gagged. Imagine, shut up behind a wall for fifty years, and it would have been longer if those old boilers hadn't gone bad," replied the officer.

Then all the whispers started through the crowd,

"Clyde, Clyde, do you know of a Clyde from years ago?"

No one could remember because most of these people lived in the neighborhood for only five to twenty years.

"What about Mr. Sutter? He's lived here for over seventy years. He may remember something," said one of the men standing there.

"Sutter, hey, I'll tell the detectives, sir. Thank you," replied the officer.

Another woman stepped up and said, "Mr. Sutter lives in that house right over there. The one with the big Christmas tree and white window blinds. Nobody really uses blinds anymore for a front window. Most people now use curtains or shades."

The officer decided that he should take this information down. He pulled a small notepad from his shirt pocket. "What is Mr. Sutter's full name, please?" said the officer.

"Mr. William Frederick Sutter. He's a retired firefighter. My uncle John is in the same firehouse that Mr. Sutter served in. He's been retired for some time now, but he knows all about this neighborhood, he grew up here, so he knows many of the people who have lived and died here. He's probably the only one left around here who does know."

"That could be a lot of help, thank you," replied the officer.

Officer Johnny Wallace, a nice young kid two years on the force, had always had dreams of a making detective like his dad was. He believed this information could help speed up that process if he could get involved in the investigation.

A voice came from the police command car, "Wallace, I need you to clear that area and get back to headquarters."

"Yes, sir, right away, sir."

Johnny jumped in his squad car and raced off to give this info to the two detectives in charge.

Both Detective Higgins and Summers sat with Police Chief John Masters going over the case.

"This is a really strange one, Higgins. It could give the school a bad rap. I want you and Summers to give this one your full attention. I went to that school myself. To think that all this time, there was a body behind a wall. I'll tell you, some of those hallways kind of gave me the creeps as a kid. Not that I believe in ghosts or anything like that."

Just then, there was a knock on the door.

"Yeah, come on in," said the chief.

Johnny Wallace popped his head, "Sorry, Chief Masters. But I have some information for the detectives here concerning the school case."

"Come in, Johnny. What do you have?" replied the chief.

"Well, some people standing around at the school told me of a retired firefighter who has lived in the neighborhood there right across the street from the school all his life. They said that he would probably remember this kid they found. I'm figuring he may even remember some of his old classmates and teachers."

The chief looked at Johnny and smiled.

"That's pretty good thinking, son. Higgins, you and Summers head over and see if this guy remembers anything."

"Did you get a name, kid?" said Higgins.

"I sure did, Detective, his name is Billy Sutter."

"Good job, kid."

Just then, the chief's ears perked up.

"Hey, that name sounds familiar. My dad used to say that name. Use to tell us stories about a firefighter that rescued a whole family from a burning building four stories high. He told us that this Billy Sutter kept going back into that burning building and one by one brought out the whole family, even the pet dog. Summers, take a ride over to the newspaper and check any of the old archives on that event. We could dig up a led."

Just then, Johnny jumped in, "Excuse me, sir, but I could do that if you don't mind. I would love to help out on this case, that is, if the detectives here don't mind."

"It's okay with me if it's okay with them," replied the chief.

Higgins and Summers looked at each other.

"It's okay with us, we could use the help, but anything you dig up, kid, you share with us and the chief here, understand?" said Higgins.

"Yes, sir, thank you, sir."

"And don't call me, sir. It's Higgins and Jackie."

"Yes, sir. I mean, Higgins."

The chief just laughed, shaking his head. They all exited the chief's office and headed for the parking garage.

"Johnny, you see what you can dig up from the newspaper, me and Jackie will head over and talk to this Billy Sutter fellow. Meet us back here by three. And Johnny, you might want to get into some street clothes and out of that uniform. It's easier approaching people if they see you coming in plain clothes."

"Yes, sir. I mean, Higgins."

Johnny jumped in his car and headed for home first to change clothes before heading to the newspaper. As Higgins and Jackie approached their car, Jackie leaned on the top of the car and said to Higgins, "Do you think it's a good idea to use this kid in a case like this?"

"I don't know yet. But I got a good feeling about this kid, and I usually like to go with my gut feeling. Come on, let's go visit Mr. Sutter and take a trip down memory lane."

The old one-level house at 875 Tompkins Avenue looked as manicured as the day it was built. The sidewalk leading up to the front door had beautiful mums on both sides, the windows with their hanging planters and English ivy almost touching the ground. There was a tall cypress tree on the front lawn with pine cones lying on the ground. The front windows still had the old-style venation blinds. Higgins and Jackie rang the doorbell. From inside, they could hear footsteps approaching. When the door opened, Higgins and Jackie were greeted by a young twelve-year-old girl. She was very slender with blonde hair and blue eyes.

"Can I help you?" she asked.

"Hello, miss, my name is Detective Higgins, and this is Detective Summers. We would like to see Mr. Sutter. Does he live here?"

"Yes, he is my grandfather, won't you please come in, and I'll go get him for you. He's in the study doing some writing. He does a lot of that since he retired. Please sit down."

"Thank you," replied Jackie.

As they waited in the living room, they noticed all around the room pictures of family and friends. There were awards and plagues from the fire department for bravery which took up a whole wall. Higgins and Jackie just looked at each other.

"Wow, this guy must have been something in his day. Look at all these honors," said Jackie.

"Can I help you, Detectives?" came a kindly voice from behind them.

Higgins and Jackie stood up, and standing there was Billy Sutter. A tall man with blue eyes like his granddaughter's. His blonde hair had turned shiny silver. He still carried himself well as if he were ready to go fight fires.

"Mr. Sutter, I'm Detective Higgins, and this is Detective Summers. We would like to ask you some questions if you don't mind."

"Yes, of course, Detectives. I imagine it's about what's going on across the street at the school?"

"I'm afraid so, Mr. Sutter."

"Well, sit down, Detectives, what would you like to know?"

Jackie leaned forward, holding a photo of the body but didn't show it yet, and asked, "Have you ever heard the name, Clyde Butcher?"

"Yes, I have, as a matter of fact. Every school has its bully. Clyde was ours. I don't think he ever had any friends. No one wanted to be around him. He just bullied everyone that came in his path. I didn't think about it then, but it was as if he had to prove something to everybody. He had this huge chip on his shoulder. But like any bully, when someone stands up to them, they back down. He tried to bully me one day in the schoolyard. My dad always told me to stand up for what was right, which is probably why I became a firefighter. Anyway, he started pushing me around in front of all the girls, of course. What he didn't expect was that I pushed back. My dad had me take martial arts at a young age. I just didn't go around broadcasting it. Clyde went to throw a punch at me, and I blocked it and threw him against the school wall and started pounding his face in. The teachers had to run over and break us up. We both landed in the principal's office. He never bothered me after that. That didn't stop him from bullying the other kids. Then one day, he didn't show up for school. And no one ever saw him again. We all figured he had moved and gone to another school. The thing is. Nobody cared. Clyde was gone, and everyone could now live a normal life. And he was forgotten."

That's when Higgins got up, walked over to the window, peeked through the blinds, and said, "Well, Mr. Sutter, Clyde did move. He moved into the boiler room of that school, behind a block wall. Tied to a school chair and gagged. And that's where he's been for the last fifty years."

Billy got up and walked over to the detective.

"Are you telling me somebody killed him?"

"That's what I'm saying, Mr. Sutter," replied the detective.

Just then, Billy remembered something.

"If you could gather this information and meet us downtown at our office, we would appreciate it," said Higgins.

"I can be there tomorrow at around noon. And please, call me Billy."

Meanwhile, at the local newspaper office, Johnny sat at a computer going over old articles related to Billy Sutter. Johnny was impressed by how many firefighters gave their lives in the line of duty rescuing people from burning buildings and car accidents. Then Johnny came across an article with a photo of a firefighter climbing down a hook and ladder carrying a person on his shoulder. The ladder must have been forty feet in the air. There was black smoke billowing out of the windows and flames shooting up from the rooftop. And there, in the middle of all this, was Billy Sutter. Then Johnny noticed a video. He clicked on it, and there were reporters all around this burning building. Suddenly, from a cloud of smoke, came three firefighters holding a man, a woman, and one carrying a small child from the building. As the last firefighter came near the camera holding the child, Johnny could see again that this was Billy Sutter. Johnny just leaned back in the chair and thought, *Boy, I should have become a firefighter*. He needed to get this information back to the office. Turning off the computer, he jumped up and flew out of the newspaper office.

The rain was coming down in buckets the next day. Higgins and Jackie sat discussing their conversation with Billy and holding the articles that Johnny had brought them. Each had a cup of coffee in hand with the sound of rain beating against the window. Suddenly, the door opened, and in came Johnny with Billy right behind him. Billy carried a briefcase under his arm as they entered.

"Good afternoon, Billy. What do you have for us?" asked Higgins.

"I have names, numbers, pictures, yearbook, teachers who are still alive, I think, and one IOU," replied Billy.

"Wow, maybe you need to come out of retirement and come and work for us," said Jackie.

Then Billy noticed the articles on the desk.

"Looks like you have been doing your homework as well."

"Not us, Johnny got these from the newspaper. Judging from these articles, you are quite the hero, Billy."

Billy just blushed a bit and said, "We are all heroes, Detective. Anyone who goes out of their way to help another that needs help is a hero in my book. You know, young Wallace's Uncle Sunny worked in the same firehouse with me back in the seventies. He saved my butt a few times. He was a good firefighter, but we lost him to that big brush fire up by the canyon. Saved my butt a few times. But enough about me. I hope all this stuff can help you. Many of the kids in this yearbook knew Clyde or had some kind of altercation with him."

Jackie took the yearbook from Billy and started skimming through the pages. It was odd, looking at all these kids from the sixties with their long hair and beehive hairdos. Then suddenly, they came to Clyde Butcher. They now had a face to match the body. There he was in all his dark glory: dark black hair still in a pompadour and black leather jacket, dark black eyes. He looked as if he was trying to grow a mustache. But of all the kids living in the sixties, this kid was living in the fifties trying to be Marlon Brando. It was then that Billy pointed to a kid at the top of the page.

"This kid here. He had a few issues with Clyde, Roger Butler. Clyde was always stealing this kid's lunch money and embarrassing him in front of the girls. I used to stand there and watch as Clyde walked away, the look on this kid's face, if looks could kill, boy Clyde would have disintegrated into thin air as he walked down the hall. Roger hated him. But then Roger was an honor student. Told everyone he would be a doctor someday. And he did. He is one of the top heart surgeons in the country today."

Higgins just looked at Jackie and then looked at Billy.

"Where can we find him?"

Billy looked at them and smiled.

"Now that! I know. He was at the reunion. I believe he lives in Philly."

"What do you say, Jackie, up for a flight to Philly to see the good doctor?"

"I think I'll stay here and check out more of these students with Billy. Why don't you take Johnny there? It will be a good learning experience."

"Let's go, kid, class time."

Johnny's face just lit up.

"Thanks, Jackie."

Jackie just gave Johnny the wink.

"Okay, Billy, let's see what other surprises this yearbook holds," said Jackie.

The case was starting to get hot now. This yearbook could be a treasure trove of information about who put an end to Clyde Butcher and his reign of terror. The rain started beating heavy on the windows. There was a burst of thunder as Jackie and Billy went through the old school pictures. As Higgins and Johnny went to see the chief about the plane fare to Philly, Billy suddenly pointed to another student. This time, it was a girl, Jenny Lipton. As Jackie stared at the picture, she could almost see herself at that age. She wasn't a pretty girl, to say the least. Kind of homely, but she had a nice face, straight brown hair, no makeup, and a little heavy set.

"I know that there was something going on between Clyde and her. They would disappear sometimes. Nobody knew where they went, but they soon returned to class in time."

"Was she at the reunion?" asked Jackie.

Billy had to think about that. If she was, he probably didn't recognize her. Then again, she could have been the prettiest one there.

"Let me call one of the other people that I know who were at the reunion. Maybe they will know if she was there or not," said Billy.

Just then, Billy's cell phone rang.

"Hi, Grandpa, we were supposed to go to the park and do some birding together, remember?"

"Ah, yes, I'll be right home, Susan. Give me about twenty minutes," replied Billy.

Billy looked at Jackie. "That was my granddaughter, Susan. I promised her we would go bird-watching today. She loves birds. Plus, she wants to break in her new digital camera. I have to go. You try to find Jenny."

And out the door, Billy went to meet Susan. Jackie turned to her computer and started the search.

"Okay, Jenny Lipton, let's see if you are still around here. And what you and Clyde were up to."

As Jackie looked through the yearbook at all those sixties faces, she began to have flashbacks of an earlier time in her own life during those school years when she was the fly on the wall. The one nobody ever asked out or wanted to make friends with. Sure, she was also an honor student. She always dreamed of working in law enforcement. Dating wasn't the first thing on her mind like all the other girls, many of who got pregnant at an early age. No! She was going to put criminals in jail. But as time went on, she gracefully turned into a very pretty young woman. She eventually had to learn to say no to some suitors who came around trying to turn on the charm. They all wanted marriage. But Jackie's job came first. At least for now, she was still a junior detective, and there was still a lot to learn before she even thought about making babies.

Skimming through the old pictures in the yearbook, she looked up, and seeing herself in a reflection in a picture of her mom on her desk, she turned toward the rain beating on the window, then said to herself, "Nope, not yet, Jackie. These girls in this yearbook are all grandmothers now. Not yet, kid. You still got ways to go before you think about that. So let's find out where you are, Jenny Lipton."

And with that thought, Jackie turned to her computer and started getting down to business. Gazing at the computer, about thirty Jenny Lipton's came up in all different places.

"Okay, let's find the ones in their seventies. Here's one. Seattle, Washington. That's a good name. No phone number. Okay, let's find your next of kin. Tommy Lipton. Phone number, ah! Here it is. Okay, Tommy, Let's see if you know where mommy is."

Jackie picked up the phone and started dialing. The phone kept ringing and ringing.

"Hi, this is Tom Lipton, I can't come to the phone right now, please leave a message, and I'll call you back. Thanks."

"Hello, Tom, this is Detective Jackie Summers of the Albany Police. I need to ask your sister some questions about a classmate she went to school with. Please call me back on this number, and I will give you some details of the case. I really need to speak with her."

Billy drove up to the house, and as he neared the garage, Susan came running out.

"Grandpa, your back. Are you ready to go find some cool birds?"

"Yes, I am Susan. Do you have your trusty camera with you?" replied Billy.

"It's right here."

"Okay then, let's go get some pictures of some cool birds."

Billy loved going with Susan on these outings. Sometimes Billy would have his daughter Melody join them. They all loved the outdoors.

The rain had stopped now and was clearing up with some small clouds hanging in the sky. There was a cool breeze coming in from the ocean, and one could smell the salty air. The path entering the park had park benches to rest, and the tall maple and oak trees towered high into the air. There were birds flying from tree to tree, chirping their beautiful songs. Squirrels scampered on the ground, hunting for nuts buried in the grass. It was the perfect day for a grandfather and his granddaughter to go bird-watching. They both walked along, cameras ready and heads tilted up, waiting for a great close-up shot.

"Grandpa, look, a beautiful red cardinal sitting on that branch a couple of inches off the stream at the water's edge."

"Okay, Susan, let's be very quiet and try to get as close as possible."

They inched their way very slowly toward the bird perched just over the water. This would be a great shot with clear water and stones just under the surface and the cardinal all in the picture. All was quiet, only the sound of running water. Susan raised her camera ever so gently and, using her zoom lens, focused on the cardinal. Its bright red wings shined in the sunlight. Once focused and clear, the only sound was "*click.*"

"Got it, Grandpa, what a shot."

They both looked at the finished product on the digital camera.

"That is a great shot, Susan. Let's go get more. There are plenty of birds flying around today. I'll bet you, we get a least two dozen great shots today."

Susan smiled with a smile only grandpas could appreciate. That day they got over three dozen great bird pictures. It was getting near dinner time, and stomachs were beginning to grumble.

"What do you say we head home, Susan, for something to eat. I'm sure your mom is cooking up something great as usual, and my tummy is beginning to talk to me."

They both laughed and started up the path toward the car. Halfway there, Billy's cell started to vibrate in his pocket.

"Hello, this is Billy."

"Hi, Billy, this is Detective Summers. I was wondering if you could come down to the office tomorrow morning. I was looking over this yearbook again, and I had some questions concerning a couple of students."

"Sure thing, Detective, I'll be there in the morning. I like my coffee black, three sugars."

"You got it, Billy, see you then," replied the detective.

Billy looked at Susan. "Well, it looks like I'm back putting out fires again."

Susan smiled, "Well, you're really good at it, grandpa."

"That's why you are my favorite granddaughter Susan."

"Grandpa, I'm you're only granddaughter."

They both walked up the path, laughing and looking at all the great pictures they had captured in the park.

The next morning proved to be another fine day with cool breezes and fresh air in from the sea. Some gulls managed to find their way inland and were hovering just over the police building. Billy stopped just before entering the building and gazed at the gulls.

"Haven't seen gulls this far inland in a while. Maybe it's an omen," he said to himself as he shrugged his shoulders and entered the building. As he walked into the detective's area, there was Detective Summers holding a fresh cup of black coffee with three sugars.

"Good morning, Billy, good of you to come this morning. I was wondering if you could help me with one of these students I came across in the yearbook."

"Always happy to help, Detective."

As Billy raised his cup to take a sip, the detective pointed to a picture in the yearbook. The coffee didn't make it to his lips. He lowered the cup, staring at the face in the yearbook. The detective noticed the look right off. Billy just stared at the face. A face he hadn't seen in over fifty years. It was a girl with long brown hair, green eyes, and a flawless complexion. The name below "Rosemarie Palazzo."

As he stared at Rose's face, images of the past began racing through his mind. There were flashbacks of the time they sat on the hood of his car by the lake, watching the moon come up sharing chicken chow mein out of those white to-go boxes. Then the high school dance, as they held each other in the center of the dance floor, slow dancing to Dupree's song, "You Belong to Me." And the day Rose and her family were getting into the car moving to Oregon. The moving van was pulling away, and he stood across the street, their eyes were locked on each other for the last time. Rose's dad sat behind the steering wheel and told her, "Rose, it's time to go, sweetheart. You can write him." As she lowered herself into the back seat of the car, Rose blew Billy a kiss. It would be their last.

"Billy, are you okay? Did you know this girl?"

"I did, she was my girlfriend in high school. We dated the whole three years until her father, who was a captain in the army, got transferred to Oregon, and that was that. We talked about growing old together. We wrote to each other for months afterward. Then the letters stopped. I found out later she met some army guy her father had hooked her up with. They served in the same platoon together. Anyway, she married him. The other part of the story is Clyde was panning after her the whole while we were dating. He was always showing off in front of her, trying to make me look bad. He knew I could kick his ass if I wanted to, so he always kept his distance. What he didn't know was that she always thought of him as a real jerk, so I had nothing to worry about from him."

Billy picked up the book and gazed at Rose.

"I wonder if she is still that beautiful."

The detective grabbed a tissue and started to wipe her eyes.

"Wow, Billy, you're going to make me cry here. I didn't know there was so much drama in high school back then."

"Oh, there sure was drama, Detective, believe me. There was plenty of drama. Back then, this was like *Peyton Place*. Everybody knew everyone else's business. That's because everyone knew each other in this neighborhood. There weren't too many secrets. But to see Rose again? That's a face that will never leave my mind."

"Well, Billy, how would you like to fly with me to Oregon to visit her? I've been doing my homework here while you were out bird-watching with your granddaughter. Turns out, she still lives in Oregon. She's a widow now. Her husband died of cancer a few years ago. She has four children and ten grandchildren. I guess her husband was a farmer and rancher. She lives on a two-hundred-acre farm. So how about it, Billy, want to take a ride with me back in time? Perhaps she still has that twinkle in her eye for you after all these years."

Billy just smile and blushed a bit as he looked at the photo of Rose in the yearbook. He looked at Jackie with glassy eyes.

"I always wondered what she looked like now. If she was still alive and how she was doing. I must admit detective. I'm a bit nervous about seeing her again after all these years."

Jackie placed her hand on Billy's shoulder.

"It's only natural, Billy. Anybody would be. I was nervous about going to my five-year reunion. I can imagine what you feel not seeing your high school sweetheart after fifty years. Come with me. I want to see what happens too with you two love birds."

"All right, Jackie, I'll go. But I'm not promising you anything. She may have a boyfriend or something."

Billy kind of stammered a bit.

"You'll be fine. I'll bet you, she is still as pretty as that photo there."

Billy just looked into thin air as if in a trance. One could see what was going through his mind.

Jackie stood there, watching him. She had a huge grin on her face. This was going to be a very interesting case indeed.

The phone rang on Jackie's desk. "This is Detective Summers."

"Detective Summers, this is Pete Fargo, the medical examiner, we met at the school with Detective Higgins."

"Oh, yes, Pete. What do you have?"

"Well, Detective, after examining the body, clothes, the chair that the body was tied up in, and going over the evidence with my assistants, we've all come up with the same conclusion. This guy was still alive when they walled him up in that hole. We found scratch marks on the arm of the chair where he tried to break free. His fingernails were worn clear down to the bone. The chair itself was fastened to the floor, so he couldn't lift it up. His legs were tied. This guy was left there to die a miserable death, and he was put there to die alone. I've seen a lot, Detective, but nothing like this one. No, this was planned and executed just the way they wanted it to. Someone got revenge. This guy must have been some piece of work, boy. Anyway, that's what we've come up with, Detective."

"Thanks, Pete, I'll let Detective Higgins know."

Jackie just hung up the phone staring off in bewilderment. Billy looking on, said, "What's up, Detective?"

"That was the medical examiner. Our guy was still alive when they walled him up in that school basement."

"What! Oh my god."

Billy just pulled up a chair and sat down, trying to grasp the idea in his head. Jackie did the same. They both looked at each other with the same dumbfounded look on their faces. This was one for the books. Who could have it in them to do such a horrible thing to another person, even if he was a bully? Jackie looked down at the photos in the yearbook. Billy came around and stood behind her, looking, too, at those faces. The faces he himself went to school with.

Meanwhile, Detective Higgins and Johnny Wallace were boarding a plane to pay a visit to Roger Butler.

"Thanks for letting me in on this case, Detective. I always wanted to see what it was like on the other side of the wall," said Johnny.

"My pleasure, kid. I had to start out the same way, working with a grumpy old detective. But I learned a lot from that guy, burping, farting, and growling stomach. Not to mention those lousy cigars he smoked."

They both laughed as they walked down the corridor toward the plane. Higgins and Johnny sat down and buckled their seatbelts. Johnny pulled out a copy of the photo from the yearbook of Roger Butler.

"Seems like a nice enough guy from the photo. Wouldn't take him for a murderer," said Johnny.

"First lesson, kid, never go by what you see in a photo. You can't tell what's going on behind someone's mind when they've been wronged. The nicest person in the world can turn when they have reached a limit and can take no more abuse. We're all capable of anything, son, when that one button is pushed."

Higgins just stared at Johnny with a serious face. Johnny just looked out the window as the plane began to back away from the platform and start down the runway. Training day had started for this lad, and on one of the toughest cases, Higgins and Summers would ever face. As the plane lifted off and ascended into the air, Johnny turned to see Higgins still looking at him.

"Are you ready for this, kid?"

"Yes, sir, I am."

"Good."

Higgins and Johnny stood outside the airport taxi area. Waving down a cab, they got in. "Jefferson Heart Institute, cabbie."

"Yes, sir, be there in ten minutes."

As they pulled up to the red brick and glass five-story building, they both eyed the building, hoping Dr. Butler was there. As they went in and walked up to the information desk, the security guard stepped up to greet them. Higgins flashed his gold shield.

"I'm Detective Higgins with New York PD, this is Officer Wallace. We're here to see Doctor Roger Butler. Do you know if he is available to see us?"

"Wait just one minute, Detective, while I call upstairs and check."

"Thank you," replied the detective.

The guard soon returned and said, "Dr. Butler is in surgery at the moment, gentlemen. But he did say that you can go up and wait in his office if you like. I just need to give you these visitor's badges if you don't mind. And you can go over to the elevator right over there and up to the third floor to room 301. His assistant will be waiting for you."

"Thank you again."

They both walked over to the elevator and stepped in. As they rode up, Johnny's heart started pounding a bit. Higgins could sense his nervousness.

"Steady lad, you'll get used to it."

"I didn't think my first interrogation would be with a prominent heart surgeon."

"It's not an interrogation, Johnny. We're just here to talk to him and see what he remembers about our guy. That's all, relax, you'll be fine."

The elevator door opened to a beautiful painting of wild stallions running along the plains with huge mountains in the background. Then turning right, they headed down the hall until they came to suite 301. Dr. Roger Butler was in big, bold letters on the smoked glass door. As they walked in, they were greeted by a pretty redhead sitting behind a large wooden desk.

"Please come in, Detectives, the doctor should be in shortly, he's just finishing up with a patient. The security guard downstairs called to say that you were on your way up. I'm Debra Butler, Dr. Butler's daughter. Please have a seat while you wait."

"Thank you, Miss Butler," replied Higgins.

Higgins motioned for them to sit. There were two plush armchairs in front of the huge window facing a large park across the street, tall trees, and sidewalks with a playground for the kids.

"It must be nice working for your father, Miss Butler."

"Yes, it is, Detective. That is until I finish medical school in four years, then I can help my father in the operating room. He's a great teacher and motivator. My mother says that I'm just like him. So I decided to become a heart surgeon myself."

"I think you will make a great heart surgeon, Miss Butler," said Johnny.

"Why, thank you, Detective."

"It's officer, Miss Butler, Officer Johnny Wallace. I'm still training with Detective Higgins."

"Well, thank you, Officer Johnny Wallace," said Debra with a smile.

Higgins just looked at Johnny with that "You dog" look.

Just then, the door opened, and in walked Dr. Butler. Both men rose to introduce themselves.

"Dr. Butler, I'm Detective Higgins, and this is Officer Wallace. Could we have a few minutes of your time, sir?"

"Of course, gentlemen. Please come into my office."

They walked into a huge room with solid oak floors. There were plaques and awards of honor all over the walls. Behind his desk were three books written by him, all on heart surgery. And on the bookshelf was a picture of him and none other than Billy Sutter.

"You and Billy Sutter must be close friends, Dr. Butler?"

"Oh, yes, that was taken at our last reunion. Billy and I go way back. He did what he always wanted to do, which was become a firefighter, and I did what I wanted to do, which was become a heart surgeon."

"Well, sir, that's the reason we're here today. To pick your brain about what you remember of your old school days. I have a photo here, I would like to see what you can tell us about him," said Higgins.

And he slid the photo from the school yearbook of Clyde Butcher.

"Wow, now there's a face from the past I didn't think I'd ever see again. Clyde Butcher. Wow. All I can tell you, Detective, is that he was a real bully in school. He used to always steal my lunch money and push me around, usually to impress some girl standing by, even if he didn't know her. No one liked him. The only one he never really bothered was Billy because he knew Billy could kick his ass, and God forbid that should happen with girls looking on. Billy was dating Rose at the time, and Clyde kept trying to impress her, even in front of Billy, but she pretty much just blew him off as a jerk. All

I know, Detective, is that one day, Clyde just never showed up at school again. Everyone thought that maybe he moved and went to another school or went to jail. I can tell you this. Everyone in that school was happy when he never came back. And I mean, everybody. Even the teachers had had enough. He was just bad news. But why all the fuss about Clyde now, after all these years?"

"Well, Doctor, Clyde never did move to the city or even go to jail. In fact, he never left the school. Some construction workers found Clyde down in the basement of the school a few days ago, walled up in an old storage room. Looks like he'd been there since you last saw him. He had a note in his pocket. It said, 'Clyde Butcher, Bully, but he'll never bully again.'"

Then Higgins slid another photo to the doctor of Clyde in the chair fifty years later. The doctor took it, and his eyes just widened as he stared at the photo of a skeleton with the clothes he remembered Clyde always wore, taking both photos in each hand and going back and forth looking at them, before and after.

"Doctor Butler, can you think of anyone from that school that hated him this much to do something like this?" asked Higgins.

The doctor looked up with a straight face and said, "Pretty much everybody in that school, Detective. I don't know how else to say it. I don't think that there was one person in that school who didn't want to punch his lights out. But you said he was walled up. Who would have that kind of experience in masonry to do that? Not any of the kids, I would guess."

"Good point, Doctor, good point. I didn't really think about that until you mentioned it. Johnny, have you been writing all this down?"

"Yes, sir, I have."

"Thank you, Doctor, for your time, sorry to have troubled you."

"No trouble, Detective. I guess you put to rest what a lot of people have been wondering for the past fifty years. And now we know. Clyde got what was coming to him."

"Thank you again, Doctor. This is my card in case you remember anything more that can help us with this case," said Higgins.

"Of course, Detective."

Higgins and Johnny shook hands with the doctor and headed for the door. As they walked through the front office, Johnny leaned over to shake Debra's hand.

"Good luck, Miss Butler, with your medical career."

"Thank you, Officer Johnny Wallace," Debra said and smiled.

As they walked to the elevator, Higgins turned to Johnny.

"You dog."

Just then, Higgins's cell phone rang.

"Higgins here."

He listened in silence for a while, then hung up and put the phone back in his pocket with a strange look on his face. At the same time, Dr. Butler came from his office heading toward the elevator when he noticed Higgins's face.

"Something wrong, Detective? You look as if someone just walked over your grave."

"I just got a call from my partner back in New York. The medical examiner just called and said Clyde Butcher was still alive when he was walled up in that chair. Someone put him in there and left him to die alone behind four block walls."

They all stood dumbfounded, not knowing what to say.

The doctor looked at Higgins and said, "That is just insane. Not even Clyde deserved a death like that. Who, in God's name, could hate someone that bad to do something like bury another human alive to die alone?"

It was something neither of them could wrap their heads around.

"Doctor, you are wanted up in the recovery room, Mr. Burk just woke up from his surgery, and the family is asking for you," came Debra's voice from the phone speaker.

"Well, gentlemen, forgive me, but I must leave you. Duty calls. We performed a triple bypass on Mr. Burk today, and I imagine he is in some pain after the surgery. I can't keep him or the family waiting. You can see your way out. My daughter can give you any of my information if you need to reach me for any more questions," said Dr. Butler.

"Of course, sir. You should get to your patient. I'll call next time if I have any more questions. Thank you for your time, Doctor," replied Higgins.

Debra sat at the desk as her father walked past her at a good pace, followed by Higgins and Johnny.

"Your father has a very demanding life, young lady, are you ready for that life?" asked Higgins.

"I've worked here for a year and a half and seen him give his all to his patients, Detective. He's a great doctor and a great father. Can I do any less than him?"

"I think you'll be a great doctor, Debra. After all, you have a great teacher," said Johnny.

"Come on, kid, we have to get back to our own stomping ground. We got a lot of work ahead of us," said Higgins.

As they left the office, Debra gave Johnny a smile of thanks. The two went over to the elevator and waited. Johnny stood gazing off down the hall. Then he walked to the end of the hall, where there was a block wall with a picture hanging on it. Higgins followed, wondering where he was going. Then standing alongside Johnny, they both just stared at the wall.

"What up, kid? What are you thinking?" asked Higgins.

"I'm thinking about what the medical examiner said about the bully being alive when he was walled up. And then I remembered my Uncle Joey did block work for a living. I used to help him during the summer. He was real good at his job. I mean, he did it for twenty years or so. It's not easy work. It's actually heavy work. Not something a high school kid could do in a few hours and do it right if you know what I mean. Look at this wall, how all the joints are perfect, and the mortar is done so well. So how does a young eighteen-year-old kid do such a good job in that basement lifting heavy blocks nine feet off the ground by himself? He had to have help, and it had to be someone who knew what they were doing."

Higgins just looked at the wall, then at Johnny.

"You know what, kid? You might have something. Pretty good detective work, son. We may have more than one killer here. Pretty good. You're learning, kid. Let's get back to the office and share this with Detective Summers."

The elevator door opened, and the two rushed to get in. As the doors closed, Higgins gave Johnny a pat on the back. Johnny felt like a detective with a slight smile. The doors closed.

Billy drove up to the house and pulled into the driveway. His daughter Melody had just pulled up a few minutes before him. She stood by the front and waved.

"Hi, Dad."

Billy got out and strolled up to Melody and gave her a hug.

"Hey, there, big girl. What brings you by this morning?"

"Well, I just dropped Susan off at her friend Lily's house to play for a while and thought I'd come by to see how the big case is going. You know, Dad, besides being a firefighter, you always had it in you to be a detective too."

Billy smiled. "I guess you know me better than I know me, big girl. Come on, let's go in and have some tea and chat a while."

Billy took out a wad of keys from his pocket and opened the door. As they walked into the kitchen, Melody asked, "So, Dad, any new developments? The whole town is talking about you working with the police trying to find out who done it."

"Well! Big girl, Detective Summers wants me to go Oregon with her to question one of the students from the yearbook."

"Really, who?" replied Melody with an inquisitive smile.

"Rosemarie Palazzo."

"Rosemarie Palazzo. I remember you and Mom talking about a Rose from years ago from school. Wasn't she your—"

"Yes, she was. It was before I met your mother. But yes, we dated throughout our high school years. But then her dad got transferred to another army base in Oregon. We lost touch with each other over the years. She eventually got married. I got on the fire department, met your mom a year later, and the rest is, as they say, history."

"So where is she now?"

"From what Detective Summers has told me, she is a widow. Her husband passed away a couple of years ago, leaving her a two-hundred-acre farm. She has grown children and grandchildren that help her out on the farm. Melody, it's been over fifty years. All I've been thinking about since the detective asked me to go is what the heck do I say to my high school sweetheart after all this time. I would never change the time I had with your mother. That was the best time of my life. We talked about growing old together when we were in school. And then she was gone. Just like that. And now, to see her again."

Melody sat there with tears in her eyes.

"Dad, the time you had with Mom, was fantastic, and nobody can ever take that away from you. You have great memories of the time you had together. But Mom's gone home to be with the Lord. And maybe you should think about moving on. Hey, who knows, she might even still have that spark there for you."

"That's what Detective Summers said. I don't know about this. Maybe I shouldn't do this. My age and—"

"Now, don't give me that my age thing. You're one of the youngest men I know at your age. You've always been young at heart, Dad. Maybe she's young at heart too. Only one way to find out." Melody smiled.

"Okay, big girl. But don't blame me if she slams the door in my face."

Melody got up and kissed Billy on the top of his head.

"I love you, Daddy, got to go pick up Susan at Lily's. Keep me posted on the case and Rose."

"I will, big girl, I will."

Billy sat at the kitchen table, holding a cup of tea and looking over the mantle of family pictures and his wedding picture. He just shook his head. Then reaching for the phone, he dialed Jackie Summers.

"Detective Summers, can I help you?"

"Detective, it's me, Billy. Listen, I want to go to Oregon with you. But I don't want to go unannounced. I can't just show up at Rose's front door. Would you call first to let her know that we will be coming? I don't want any surprises. It's been too long a time in between. I want to see her face knowing that I am coming."

"I understand, Billy. There won't be any surprises. I want to see her face too. I'm as much a part of this as you are now, partner."

Billy smiled on the other end and hung up the phone.

The rain beat against the windowpane in the kitchen as Rose washed dishes, looking out across the cornfield and the horse corral. The chickens scurried around the big red barn, clucking away while rosters chased them. Benny, the golden retriever, came in and sat down next to Rose and gave a bark.

"Okay, Benny, I know you're hungry, I'll feed you just as soon as finish these dishes. Now be a good boy and go get Judy to come to help me. Go get her, boy."

Just then, Judy came into the kitchen, grabbing Benny's neck and giving him a rub.

"No need, I'm right here, boy. Hi, Mom. Let me help you dry those dishes. Don't you love the rain?"

"I sure do, sweetheart. It makes everything smell so clean after a good pouring," answered Rose. "Oh, there's the phone, I'll get it, dear."

As Rose dried her hands, she grabbed the phone. "Hello."

As Judy dried the dishes, she didn't hear any talking. She turned to see her mother standing there with a blank look on her face and staring into nowhere.

"Mom, are you all right. What is it, Mom?"

Rose didn't say anything for a moment. She just hung up the phone and looked at Judy with that blank look and said, "Billy Sutter." Rose pulled out a chair from the kitchen table and sat down, staring off.

Then she spoke, "That was a Detective Jackie Summers of the New York Police Department. She is coming here to ask me some questions about a person I went to high school with, and she is bringing Billy Sutter with her."

"Who is Billy Sutter, Mom?"

"He was my high school sweetheart, dear. We went together for three years. We were in love. Then your grandfather got transferred here to Oregon. Billy and I lost touch over the years. I met your father, and here we are. And they will be here tomorrow afternoon."

"But why is she bringing your old boyfriend to ask questions?" asked Jackie.

"Well, if I still know Billy. He loved the old neighborhood. He would never leave. And he probably still lives in the old house across the street from the school. Everybody knew each other in that neighborhood, sweetheart, and Billy probably knows more about it than most people. He's most likely helping the police in some cases. That's just how Billy was. Always trying to do the right thing. That's my Billy."

"Mom, you sound like you still have a thing for him." Judy giggled.

"Oh, you shush, go finish drying those dishes, you little stinker."

Rose got up and gave Judy a tickle in her ribs as they went back over to the sink. Rose just stared out the window with a faraway look on her face. A look that was not focused on the farm.

Jackie Summers pulled into her parking spot at headquarters. The radio blasted some rap songs. It was 6:00 a.m. Running up the steps and through the glass doors, she ran down the hall to her office. As she burst through the door, she stopped short to see Higgins, Johnny, and Billy sitting there, each with a coffee cup in their hand.

"Oh! You're all here, I thought I was late."

"You are. We were all supposed to meet here at five thirty, remember?" said Higgins.

"Sorry, got my times crossed," she replied.

Higgins sat at his desk going over the medical examiner's report, then hopping up with papers still in hand, went over to Jackie and handed her two plane tickets.

"The chief just cleared these. They're two plane tickets to Oregon. I believe the two of you need to catch a plane. It leaves in two hours from Albany Airport. Johnny and I are going to take another look at the crime scene over at the school. The kid's been doing his homework. We might find something we missed. You two better get going. Billy here has a date."

Jackie turned to Billy and noticed something different about him. He got his haircut, and he shaved. He also had on his Sunday best gray suit and shiny black shoes.

"Wow, Billy! You look dressed to kill. Going to see anyone special?" Jackie smiled.

Billy just blushed and said, "I guess I'm just old school. This is how we, old guys, dress when we are going to see our old high school sweethearts that we haven't seen in over fifty years. Nothing wrong with making a good impression, is there?"

"Of course, not Billy. You look fantastic. I wouldn't be surprised if she ran right up to you and threw her arms around you and gave you a big kiss right on the lips," said Jackie as she straightened his tie.

"Well, I guess we should be going before I change my mind," replied Billy.

Jackie motioned, "Age before beauty, sir."

All four walked down the hall and out to their cars. Higgins and Johnny jumped in the black sedan and took off toward the school. Jackie and Billy hopped in Jackie's car and started for Albany Airport. Billy looked white as they headed to the Belt Parkway. Jackie looked at Billy while trying to keep her eyes on the road.

"Billy, relax. You'll be fine. She is probably just as nervous as you. Remember, she hasn't seen you in fifty years either."

"I guess you're right. There's nothing to be nervous about, right? We're grown adults and should act accordingly," said Billy as he looked at Jackie, his legs shaking a mile a minute.

Jackie just looked and smiled a big smile and said under her breath, "Oh, my goodness, I feel like I have my sixteen-year-old nephew in the car."

"Did you say something?"

"I said, after all this, I have to go to a bar," replied Jackie.

Soon they were boarding the plane. As they walked down the walkway to the plane, Billy was silently nearing the door to the plane.

"Relax, Billy. You would think you were walking *The Green Mile*," said Jackie.

"I'm okay now. I'll be fine," he replied.

They took their seats, and in a few minutes, they were in the air.

"We should be there by 1 p.m. I have a rental car waiting for us at Hertz. Remember, we are going to see if she remembers anything about this Clyde fella. We need to stay focused, Billy. All the mushy stuff comes second. Once we get all the information from all these students that knew him, then we can start to put the pieces together and find out who put him behind that wall. I still get the chills just thinking about it, being tied up, gagged, and walled up alive. I would have just got my big brother to kick the shit out of him and left it at that. Believe me, once my brother got hold of him, he wouldn't ever bully anybody ever again."

"Was your brother a fighter?" asked Billy.

"He was a Navy SEAL. He was always watching out for me. Always check out any boys I brought home. Made sure I stayed in school. Didn't cut out or anything like that. He was my guardian angel."

"What happened to him?"

"We were at the beach one day with my mom swimming. A little kid got caught in an undertow and pulled out into the deep water. When my brother heard his mother screaming, he did what he was trained to do. He went out to save him. He managed to reach the kid and hold on to him. As he swam back, a huge wave came in and picked up my brother and the boy and threw them against the pier pillion. He was killed instantly. The boy held on to his body as other rescuers swam out and brought them in. The boy was fine, just some water in his lungs. But my brother died saving that boy. That's why I know he is always still with me, my guardian angel. And since you're with me on this case. He is yours too."

"Now, I don't feel nervous at all. Wow, it's as if my nerves just calmed down. I feel confident, ready to take on the world. I have a guardian angel now. Okay, Jackie, let's do this," replied Billy.

Higgins and Johnny made the right turn on Chestnut Street when Higgins got a notion.

"Hey, Johnny, does your uncle still do block work?"

"He's retired, but he still does side jobs once in a while. Why?"

"Think he'd like to take a ride to the school with us and look at that wall? It would be nice to get a professional opinion on how that wall was built," said Higgins with a police-like smile.

"He doesn't live far from here. I'm sure he wouldn't mind. He's been bored stiff since he retired. It would be nice to get him out of the house. Take a left at the next light and head up to Mercer Lane, he lives right down the road from the drug store."

They pulled up in front of the house and saw Uncle Joe sitting on the front porch smoking his pipe and Sandy, his pit bull, sitting right next to him. When they got out, Uncle Joe stood to see Johnny walking up the sidewalk with Higgins right behind him. Sandy ran down the stairs to greet Johnny as he bent down to grab her neck and give her a good rub around the collar.

"Sandy's okay. She's old and just wants to get petted. She doesn't even bark that much anymore."

Higgins followed Johnny up onto the porch. Walking over to his uncle, he gave him a big hug.

"Hello, Uncle Joe, how are you? Nice to see you relaxing out here on the front porch. It's a beautiful morning."

"It is, Johnny. Sandy likes it. We sit out every morning to beat the time. Who's your friend there?"

"Oh, this is Detective Higgins, I'm helping him work on a big case that happened over at the high school."

"Oh yes, I heard about that. The whole town is buzzing about it. Jimmy over at the barber shop told me about it. Boy, who'd thought something like that could happen in this sleepy little town?"

"It's not sleepy anymore, Uncle Joe."

"I know, but it was when I was a kid growing up here. Anyway, it's nice to meet you Detective Higgins. What brings you out this way anyway?"

"Well, we need your expertise in block work. We were wondering if you would like to come with us to the school to look at the crime scene. You could be a great help," said Johnny.

"Wow, me helping on a crime investigation. I would love to help. I'm going nuts sitting around here playing the retired old guy. Let me get my jacket and put Sandy in the house, and we can be off to the crime scene."

"I told you he'd love to go. Makes him feel wanted again, you know?'

"I do. I had an uncle who went through the same thing. It's not easy to retire just like that kid. Especially when you've worked fifty or sixty years of your life with your hands and then just stop. Some people don't make it past their second year after retirement. They don't have a family to come and visit them. They just wither away and die. It's a good thing your uncle still has you."

Johnny looked at his uncle coming down the stairs as they waited by the car. He was glad to see his uncle in good spirits. It made him feel as if he knew that Uncle Joe would be around for a while.

"My uncle tries to keep himself busy doing things around the house and helping others. It keeps him in shape. Not bad for a guy of eighty-five."

Higgins nodded his head in approval as Uncle Joe met them at the car. They got in and headed for the high school. It wasn't a far ride, just a few miles on the highway. In a few minutes, they arrived and pulled up alongside the caution tape barrier that surrounded the outside doorway that led down to the basement. There were still some police officers standing around to make sure no one went in unless they had a badge or some ID. As they got out, one of the officers recognized Johnny.

"Hey, Johnny, what are you doing with the detectives?" I didn't recognize you without your uniform."

"I'm helping the detectives work on this case. The chief wants me to learn the ropes, so I'm in training with Detective Higgins here. This is my Uncle Joe. He's here to give some professional advice about the crime scene. Uncle Joe, Detective, this is Officer Danny Smith. We usually work the events together."

Uncle Joe stood tall looking important like he belonged there.

"Well, good for you, Johnny. I always knew you would make detective someday, you got it in ya, kid," said Officer Smith.

"Thanks, Danny. We're going to go down to the basement and look around. Catch you later, okay?'

"Sure thing, Johnny, maybe I'll see you over at the pub later. I owe you a beer."

As they came to the basement door, another young officer stood by and looked at Danny for approval. Danny raised his hand and gave the okay for him to let them into the basement. It was a musty smell as they entered the boiler room. There were two big old boilers that had been heating the school for over seventy years. The old oil smell that lingered on the walls was hard not to choke. As they went over to the wall where the body was found, Uncle Joe immediately noticed something odd. Bending down to examine the bottom, three blocks served as the base; he noticed that they were different from the other blocks of the existing wall. They were also a different shade. Then he pulled off a little screwdriver from his pocket and started to scrape the mortar from the existing block wall and then from the wall that fell. Then looking at some of the blocks lying on the floor, he noticed that some of them didn't break apart from the fall, which meant that the mortar was a lot stronger than the original wall. Higgins and Johnny just watched as Uncle Joe looked over the whole area like a detective. The man knew his job, and they could see he went over the scene with a fine-tooth comb. Then rising to his feet, holding a chunk of mortar from the existing wall and the fake wall, he walked over to Higgins and Johnny.

"We have here two different types of mortar. This one from the old existing wall is an interior type of mortar for inside walls. This other type of mortar you see here is an exterior mortar much stronger, meant to last. For something like this, whoever did this didn't need this type of mortar to do the job. They went through a lot of trouble to make sure this bully was never found. And judging from the joints, they made it look like it was part of the original wall, so you couldn't tell them apart. Pretty good work if you ask me. Someone knew what they were doing on this one."

Higgins and Johnny just looked at each other. Johnny's hunch was right. Whoever put Clyde Butcher behind that wall had to have planned it. They had to have all the materials down there beforehand and knew how much time they would need to finish the job. What they didn't plan on was a remodel job fifty years down the road. Or Clyde would have been forgotten about forever. Now they narrowed some of the suspects down, but they still had a long way to go. Their investigation had just started. What Higgins and Johnny needed to do was get back to the office and dig deep into that yearbook and check out every student, teacher, and custodians who had any contact with Clyde Butcher. And who would have a motive to kill him?"

"Thank you, Mr. Wallace. You have brought us a little closer to solving this puzzle," said Higgins as he shook Uncle Joe's hand.

"My pleasure, Detective. I'm glad I was able to help. And I was glad to get out of the house. We kind of helped each other," replied Uncle Joe.

"Come on, kid, let's get Uncle Joe home and us back to the office. I want to go over that yearbook with a fine-tooth comb-like Uncle Joe here. Perhaps we can dig something up on one of these people to connect the dots. I want to check if anyone in that yearbook has any prior arrests, and if so, for what. I also want to pay this Jenny Lipton a visit in the near future and ask her some questions. Billy seems to think that Clyde and this Jenny girl had something going on. I want to find out what. Someone in that yearbook must know something, or everyone is keeping this whole thing a secret. We need to start digging deep, Johnny. Now, this is where you earn your wings, kid. You find out where Jenny Lipton lives. I'm going to start digging through that yearbook to see who is still dead or alive and where they live, and if they will talk to us, even if I have to use a shoehorn to get it out of them."

"I'm on it, boss. Let's get Uncle Joe home first. He looks tired," said Johnny, laughing.

As they left the basement and walked over to the car, Johnny waved to Danny standing by his squad car.

"Danny, I'll see you later. Say hi to Jill and the kids for me."

"Will do, Johnny. Be careful, kid," replied Danny.

They all jumped in the car and drove off toward Uncle Joe's house.

Then Uncle Joe said from the back seat, "You may want to check with the registrar of contractors. They have records of masons going back years. You may be able to get a lead on any block workers that lived in the area at the time and check to see if any are still alive. He would have to have been young at the time. Also, supply house's that sold that block and mortar. Sometimes the guys that work those places remember clients, especially if they bought a lot from them.

They also would have to be young at the time. We're talking fifty years here, guys."

Higgins and Johnny knew this wasn't going to be easy. Chances are, many of these people were dead or in nursing homes. Their best chance was the students and teachers. So far, the only people they knew from that era were Billy and Uncle Joe. They had to start talking to people before they all died off.

Jackie and Billy drove along the beautiful country road in Haines, Oregon. There were tall Douglas firs, Atlas cedar, big-leaf maple, cherry, black oak, and cottonwood. They passed beautiful farms with Longwood fences and horses running out in the field. Huge barns, cornfields, hayfields, and green hills ran for miles. Just ahead, they could see a driveway with a huge wooden entrance and a long dirt road. Above the entrance in big western lettering said, "Masters Ranch." They pulled up to the entrance, paused a bit, and stared up at the sign. Both looked at each other.

"Well, Billy, this is it. The moment of truth. You ready?" asked Jackie.

"As ready as I'll ever be. Let's do it."

They started up the long dirt road past a big cornfield, and then they drove by a horse corral with about twenty horses grazing. As they turned a corner, their first view was a big red barn with a flying eagle weather vane on top. Just next door was a rustic two-story farmhouse, like something out of a picture book. There was a front porch that wrapped around the house with rockers and a swing that hung from the rafters. Out front was a Silverado pickup with a bale of hay in the back. They pulled up to the front porch, got out, and walked slowly up to the front door. Billy checked himself, and then Jackie checked him to make sure his tie was straight. Inside, they could hear a dog barking. It sounded like a big dog. Jackie knocked, and in a few moments, the door opened. Rose stood there in a beautiful red dress, her silver hair down shoulder length with a gold necklace and a cross hanging. Both Billy and Rose stood for a moment, gazing at each other. Rose was still as beautiful as ever, and Billy still with that look of love on his face as if they never were apart. Rose stepped forward, and all she could say was "Billy," then threw her arms around him and kissed him on the lips. Jackie just stood back and enjoyed every second of this. It was hard holding back tears. Rose, still with her arms around him, pulled back a bit.

"I didn't think I would ever see you again. After the letters stopped, I knew we would have to go our separate ways. But a lot has happened since then. We have much to talk about. Oh, I know you're here to ask me about Clyde. We get the news here too. I saw it on TV. Please come in, I have coffee on. Oh, I'm sorry, Detective, forgive me for not introducing myself at first, but seeing Billy, well, you understand."

"That is quite all right, Rose. Billy and I have gotten to know each other pretty well since we started this case. He told me all about your high school days. He was pretty nervous when I asked him to come with me. But now, seeing the way he looks at you and you at him, especially after that greeting at the door, I think it was well worth the wait."

"Well, why don't we have coffee. You can ask your questions. Then let me show you the farm. There is a lot to see. My son Jeffery should be here in a little while from plowing. I'd like you to meet him. And I think he would like to meet Billy. I told Jeffery all about Billy and me years ago after my husband died. He always wanted to meet the man who could have been."

Billy and Jackie sat at the kitchen table as Rose brought over the coffee cups and poured the coffee. She then set out some freshly made coffee cake. Billy took one sip. "Wow, I don't think I have ever had a better cup of coffee.

"Try the coffee cake," said Rose.

Billy took one bite, and his eyes lit up. Jackie also tried the cake and looked at Billy.

"Boy, Billy, how did you ever let this one get away?"

Billy and Rose blushed, trying not to stare at each other.

"So, Detective, what did you want to ask me about Clyde?"

"I guess anything you can remember about him and the people he bullied will help the investigation to find out who put him behind that wall," replied Jackie.

When Rose heard the wall, she cringed in her chair. Looking at Jackie, she could only imagine the sight when they found him.

"Was he really in there all these years? My god, even someone like Clyde Butcher didn't deserve a death like that. The only one he was afraid of was Billy because he knew Billy could kick his butt. But Billy would never pick a fight, although he would jump in to protect the weaker person being bullied. My friends and I always believed that someone bigger and stronger would come along one day and give Clyde a beating in front of the whole school. One he would never forget, and perhaps he would stop the bullying. Or maybe join the army and go fight where we needed fighting. Then maybe he'd get his oats out."

"What about any of the other students? Were there any that he picked on more than others?"

"Well, I know he and Jenny Lipton had something going on. They would sometimes disappear for a while and then come back. I know she didn't like him, and she wouldn't talk about it to any of us. She was shy and really not that pretty."

"Do you think he may have had something on her and was forcing her to have sex with him?"

"Could be, we would sometimes catch her looking at other people's papers in class to get answers on the test. He may have spotted her doing that and threatened to tell the teacher. I can see him doing something like that."

Jackie took a bunch of notes while Rose told what she could remember of who Clyde used to pick on the most. Billy just sat there and drank his coffee, just looking at Rose having flashbacks of yesteryear. He still could not believe that she was sitting right next to him after all these years. She still had the same smile and twirled her hair with her finger. Once in a while, Rose would glance at him as she spoke, noticing him looking at her. She knew what was going through his mind because the same thoughts were going through her mind as well. The love of her life sat right next to her after all these years, both married, both widow and widower, both with children and grandchildren. Now what? After Jackie and Rose were finished with the questions, Rose invited them to see the farm.

"Let me show the farm. My son should be here soon. He runs it now. He's a good son, hardworking and loyal to his family and the townspeople here. They all know him. And he's a volunteer firefighter." She looked at Billy and smiled.

"I like him already," said Billy.

They walked out the back door to gaze upon a beautiful two-hundred-acre spread of corn, cotton, and wheat. The house sat up on a hill, so the whole crop could be seen from up high. The bottom land always gave a good crop because the water held in the soil better. Over on the east end of the farm was a huge coral, where thirty horses ran and grazed in the most beautiful green grass. Just behind the house was a large chicken coop where Rose would gather fresh eggs every day. Folks from around the town would come by from time to time to buy some eggs. Over on the west side of the farm was a section fenced off for cattle. There were forty cows, twelve calves, and four bulls, which they sometimes studded out to other farmers in the area. There were tall oaks, maple, apple, chestnut, and pears trees surrounding the farm. One could never go hungry here. This place was right out of a storybook of home and garden. Jackie noticed the large porch with rocking chairs and a two-seated swing hanging from a beam.

"Why don't you two take a stroll and catch up while I sit here and rock while I go over my notes."

Billy looked at Rose and held out his hand. She didn't hesitate. She took Billy's hand, and off they went down the dirt path toward the horse corral. Jackie watched the two old lovebirds walk slowly down the path, taking in the surrounding sights. "You look great, Rose, you haven't changed one bit."

"Neither have you, Billy. A bit older perhaps, but still my Billy. I wanted to write more, but my father wouldn't have it. 'We were in Oregon now, and you have to put Billy out of your head,' my dad would constantly tell me. And my mom would not go up against my father. Military, you know, can't break the chain of command. Then my father brought this guy home one day for dinner. His name was Ron Masters. A captain in my father's platoon. He was a really nice guy. Very polite, always getting my chair and opening the car door for me. Eventually, we started dating, and before I knew it, we were heading to the Bahamas on our honeymoon. It all went so fast. Before I knew it, I was pregnant with my son. This farm used to belong to Ron's grandfather. He inherited it when his grandfather died. His whole family is farmers. Many of them still live here in the valley. Time has just gone by so fast, I never thought I would ever see you again, but here you are, standing in front of me, my Billy."

Rose threw her arms around him and held him close to her as if she would never let go. Then she kissed him with a long, loving kiss as if time had never passed between them. Jackie watched from the porch, tears in her eyes and a great big smile on her face. Billy held Rose's face with both hands, looking intensely into her eyes. He scanned her whole face, then pushed her hair over her ear and kissed her on the lips, then looked at her again and said, "Eat your heart out, Clyde."

Meanwhile, back at the office, Higgins and Johnny were busy going over their own notes and checking records of students from the yearbook and also any teachers who may still be alive. Then Johnny put the yearbook down and said to Higgins, "Hey, what about the custodian that worked at the school at the time. I wonder if he is still around. Maybe he could tell us something about the school boiler room and this Clyde fella?"

"Good point, kid, that's your assignment for today. See if you can dig up anything on the people that worked maintenance or even grounds people who may remember anything about the school or Clyde."

"I'm on it, boss. I'm going over to the school to check any old records they might have. We may come up with a lead," replied Johnny.

"Okay, kid. And check to see who did their masonry work. They should have old receipts or something tucked away."

Johnny bolted out the door, eager to get a lead on anything or anyone that connected to Clyde Butcher's death. Meanwhile, Higgins busied himself with the yearbook, looking at each face that stared back at him.

"Okay, which one of you little devils put the kibosh to Mr. Butcher?"

Higgins sat there for hours trying to put up anything on the computer about each student. Some had died. Some moved away to other countries. Many lived in other states. Only a few had parents still living, although they would be in their nineties and not remember too much. After about three hours, Higgins decided to try focusing on any teachers that may still be alive. Thumbing to the teacher's section of the book, he began researching the backgrounds of all the teachers to see if any of them did any kind of extracurricular work on the side, such as a trade like masonry. There were a lot of teachers at this school, but one jumped out at Higgins, who was still alive and lived not too far away. Richard Peterson was the school's gym teacher. He had been there since 1948 and probably knew most of the students. Then again, he didn't want to just narrow it down to male students. Women can be just as dangerous as men, so he browsed the yearbook to find the women's gym teacher. *Ah, Mrs. Linda Bloom. Now to see if she is still alive and kicking.* Higgins found her address on the computer. She lived in the next county within driving distance.

He thought to himself, *This could be a chance to get two birds with one stone.* Richard Peterson would be first on the list to visit. Grabbing his car keys and hat, he dashed out the door to his car and headed to see Mr. Peterson. Hopefully, he would be in a talking mood. It wasn't a far drive, just about ten miles over by the new mall. Higgins pulled up alongside a nice little cottage with a picket fence and a tall oak in the front yard. Outside was Mr. Peterson mowing the lawn with an old push mower. He looked in pretty good shape, judging from his appearance. A bit aged, of course, but still active from the looks of him. Pulling over to the curb and parking, he got out, walked over to the fence, and called to him.

"Hello, there, sir, looks like you know your way around a lawn, pretty good job."

"Thank you. I have been doing it for over seventy years and with this very same push mower," Mr. Peterson replied.

"That's amazing. You look pretty fit. I guess this must keep you in shape."

"It does, it does, but I still try to exercise when I can. That's what I used to do, you know. I was a gym teacher for over fifty years."

"Well, sir, that's why I am here. My name is Detective Gerald Higgins, and I am investigating a murder case that happened over fifty years ago at your school. I was wondering if you had time to talk, maybe jog your memory a bit."

"Certainly, Detective. Come in the house and have some coffee, and we can talk."

Higgins followed Mr. Peterson into the kitchen. It looked as if it hadn't changed since it was built. It still had all the old cabinets and windows. The curtains had little flowers, and he still used his old coffee pot. There was no microwave or dishwasher. He still had the old linoleum flooring. Higgins felt like he was in a *Leave it to Beaver* house. But it was a nice feeling to be in a time capsule like this. On the counter was a picture of his wife. The picture looked like it was taken some years ago when she was in her thirties.

"That was my Betty. She was thirty-five there. She went to be with the Lord five years ago. I do get to see my children and grand-children from time to time."

Sitting down and handing Higgins a cup of coffee, he asked, "So, Detective, what would you like to ask me. I hope I can remember back fifty years ago."

"Do you recall a student by the name of Clyde Butcher?"

"Wow, that's a name I haven't heard of in a very long time, but yes, I do remember him. Not very good memories, I'm afraid. He was something of a problem child. None of the other students liked him. He was pretty much a bully. He was always acting up in gym class, very uncontrollable. He was a bad egg from the time he entered that school till the time he left. Is he a suspect in your case, Detective?"

"No, sir, he is the victim. Some construction workers found his body behind a wall in the basement of the school while remodeling the boiler room. He was tied to a chair, gagged, and left there fifty years ago, and they just found him now."

"You mean he was left in there alive?"

"That's what it looks like. According to the medical examiner."

"It's strange now that I think about it. He was there, and then he wasn't there anymore. Most people just thought he moved away and went to another school or went into the army with the Vietnam War going on. But you know, people like that who make a point not to like others, and once they are gone, they are not even given a second thought. They just fade away like an echo. That is probably why no one ever missed him."

Higgins thought about it for a minute, sipping his coffee, then agreed.

"Ever notice Clyde bothering anyone in particular more than others?"

"I really can't remember, Detective. He bothered everyone, even teachers disliked him. Many teachers were happy when he was gone, and they didn't really care. There was one student in my class that Clyde left alone. His name was Billy Sutter. A good kid. Had good grades, good in gym, and was a popular kid at school. I think he became a firefighter after graduating. Clyde never bothered him, maybe because he met his match," replied Mr. Peterson.

"Well, as a matter of fact, Mr. Sutter is helping us on this case. He has given us a lot of information concerning the school and some of the students. He is in Oregon right now with my partner interviewing one of the former students."

"That was Billy, always trying to help the underdog."

"Yes, I'm beginning to see that. Glad he is on our side," replied the detective.

Billy and Rose leaned up against the white wooden fence of the horse corral gazing out at the beautiful stallions grazing in the field. It was so serene and peaceful, with the oaks blowing in the wind. The mountains in the background stood majestic and overpowering. Rose's hair glistened as the sun went down behind the mountain, making her glow as Billy stared at her as if he were looking at an angel. Rose turned, gazing back at him.

"What?"

"You're as beautiful as the day we met Rose. You know. I never stopped loving you. Even after I got married. Oh, I loved my wife, and I still do. But I never stopped loving you. I always wondered how you were, where you were, and if you were doing well."

"I never stopped loving you either, Billy. And I thought the same thing about you. Although, I always knew you would become a firefighter. You never stopped talking about it. And I'll bet you were the best you could be. You always did things a hundred and fifty percent. And now here you are, helping the police solve this case about Clyde's murder. A guy nobody liked. And retired, at that. Don't you ever stop?"

"I guess I'll always be me, Rose. A person has to be who they are in life, or they are living someone else's life. It's nice to do the things you want to do, but it's better to do the things you were meant to do."

The moon started to show its face just over the oaks. Now Rose's hair shined in the moonlight, and her eyes sparkled. The impulse was too great for Billy as he pulled her close and kissed her. From a distance standing on the porch, Jackie watched love in the making, shaking her head and smiling.

"Boy, some people have all the luck."

Billy and Rose strolled up the dirt path arm and arm toward the house.

"I still can't get it out of my head about Clyde, the way he died and being walled up like that alone. If they hadn't started that construction job, he would have never been found. I have been trying to remember the kids at school. If any of them were kind of strange, the only one I can think of is Jenny Lipton. She always kept to herself. Maybe because of her family life at home, I know her dad was strict, especially about boys. If he ever found out that Clyde was messing around with his daughter, he would kill him."

Billy stopped and asked, "Do you remember what her father did for a living?"

"I think he was some kind of a handyman. He was like a jack of all trades and did jobs for people in the neighborhood and in the next town. Sometimes he would get to work for a big construction company on one project then go back to his odd jobs."

"I wonder if any of those companies are still around and still have any records of their employees and what they did. This may be a lead in the case, Rose. Let's go tell Detective Summers."

As they neared the house, they could see Jackie sitting in the rocker, rocking away with her head tilted back and eyes closed. This was very different from the big city with all the street sounds. It was getting late, and everyone was tied. Jackie got up and welcomed Billy and Rose back from their walk.

"Welcome back, you two, have a nice walk together?"

The two of them cleared their throats. "Ah, yes, we did, Detective, thank you," replied Billy.

"It's getting late, Billy, we should get going to the hotel, we have an early flight tomorrow."

"Rose remembered something about Jenny Lipton's dad. He was very protective of Jenny, especially with boys. He also did construction work, a jack of all trades, she said. There could be a lead there."

"Could be. We'll tell Higgins about it when we get back to New York. You just might have something. It's funny we have been concentrating on the students and teachers. We didn't think about the parents, did we?" said Jackie.

"You're welcome to stay here if you like. I have plenty of room. All the kids are grown and gone, just me and the animals here," Rose offered.

Looking at Billy with wild oat eyes, she replied, "Thank you, Rose, but it's probably better if we go to the hotel. I'll wait for you in the car, Billy, while you two say your goodbyes."

Jackie shook Rose's hand politely and said, "It was very nice meeting you, Rose, thank you so much for your hospitality." She then walked toward the car.

Rose and Billy stood, holding each other on the porch. The moonlight beamed on both of them. Billy looked into her eyes.

"You know, I can't just say goodbye to you like this. I'll be back, Rose. We don't know how many more years we have left in this life, but I want to spend them with you. I always did."

"I will be right here when you come back, Billy."

They kissed a long kiss. The sound of the horn from the car parted their lips as Billy moved slowly from her arms toward the car. Getting in, he waved, "Keep the light on."

Rose waved at him, "I will."

Jackie started the car, and as they drove off down the dirt road, she turned to Billy. "You are one romantic Billy, I'll tell you that."

Billy smiled back. "You know, Detective. It was fate that we crossed paths on the case. It's because of you I found my Rose."

The cloud of dust followed the car as they drove off. The moonlight was just behind them.

Johnny was now on his second day at the school, going through old records and receipts of past jobs that had been done for the school by contractors. He focused on the late sixties from sixty-seven to sixty-nine. Most of the work was on the outside of the building, from changing windows to painting. Then Johnny came across a receipt for a storage closet to be built in the basement. He examined the paper closely. It was for three hundred dollars, two-block walls, five feet apart from each other with an opening for a door. But there was no name of who did the work. Apparently, the door was never put on. They just left it open. Perhaps the school couldn't afford the cost of the door and the installation. The date said April 10, 1966. So the wall was installed a year before any of those students attended. Johnny thought to himself, *Who could have done the job? It had to be someone local, someone who knew masonry.* He had to get this info back to Higgins. But first, he paid the principal's office a visit. He found the principal, Mr. Maroni, sitting at his desk, going over some papers. Poking his head in, the principal asked him to come in.

"Please, officer, come in, sit down. What can I do for you today? Find what you were looking for?"

"As a matter of fact, I found a receipt from 1966 for a block wall to be built in the basement for storage. Have any idea who it was that did the job?"

"That was long before my time, officer. I think the principal at that time was Mr. Scot Billings. I believe he passed away some nine years ago."

"Mr. Maroni, do you know of anyone still alive who might know who did the work?" replied Johnny.

Mr. Maroni scratched his head and thought for a minute. "There used to be a man, during that time, I was told that mowed our lawn and trimmed our bushes. I believe he is still alive but very old. I can't remember his name. He was the uncle of one of the students here. Sorry."

"That's okay, Mr. Maroni, I think I know someone who knows. Thank you, sir, for your time," said Johnny as he shook the principal's hand and walked out of the office.

Johnny pulled up to the police office to see Higgins when at the same time, Detective Summers and Billy pulled up alongside his car. They all got out and started for the door.

Johnny asked, "How did you make out in Oregon?"

Jackie responded, "Oh, we made out pretty good, especially Billy here. How about you? What have you been up to, Johnny?" replied Jackie.

"Well, I think I may have caught on something that might help. Let's go in and see Higgins and tell you all about it, and you can tell us what happened in Oregon."

Jackie just gave Billy that look as they walked up the stairs to the building.

They found Higgins at his desk, still looking through the yearbook. He looked up and asked, "How did it go in Oregon, Jackie? Did you make any headway?"

"We did, boss. We both did. It seems this Jenny Lipton's name keeps coming up in our interviews. Seems Clyde and her had something going on between them, although no one thinks she liked him. He may have been forcing her into something she couldn't run away from, or maybe she felt no one could help her. On the other hand, Billy here and Rose rekindled some old flames that apparently never went out."

"Well, Billy, I hope that all works out for you. How about you, Johnny? What did you dig up at the school?"

"Well, sir, I found a receipt for the walls to make that small room where they found Clyde. It was built for storage in 1966. But the principal doesn't know who did the job, it was before his time, but he does know that a man who used to do the lawn and trim the bushes there at the school is supposedly still alive, and he may remember who did the block work. I was wondering if Billy might remember."

Billy pondered the thought in his head for a minute.

"You know. There was a guy who used to mow the lawn there. He was related to one of the other students, but he wasn't that much older than us, maybe by ten years or so. He was someone's uncle. Let me see that yearbook."

Billy scanned through the yearbook, looking at each student and trying to remember. Suddenly he came to a name and a face that struck a chord.

"Here he is, Peter McCord. A skinny kid with freckles and red hair. He was always helping kids with math problems and homework assignments. An honor student. Peter got drafted in 1970. I think he was killed in Vietnam. But it was Peter's uncle that mowed the school's lawn. If he's still alive, we may find him down at the town pub. I know a lot of the old-timers around here meet there and smoke cigars and talk about Doo-Wop and the old glory days. If he's anywhere, he's there."

Higgins looked at his crew of detectives.

"Well, it's still a bit early for the pub, but why don't we go down there today around three or so and have a little chat with Mr. McCord. I may even have myself a drink with him if he gives us the information we need. In the meanwhile, we need to talk to this Jenny Lipton. It seems she knows more about this Clyde fellow than anyone. Jackie, see if you can dig up an address."

"You got it, boss. Billy, why don't you go see that granddaughter of yours. I'm sure she is wondering where grandpa has been. And maybe give a certain person a call. I'll come by around two thirty to pick you up to go see Mr. McCord. He may be willing to talk more if he sees an old face."

"That's a good idea, Jackie. You get home, Billy, and see your kids, we got some work to do here. We'll see you later," said Higgins.

"I guess I do have some thinking to do. I'll see you all later," replied Billy.

As Billy made his way to the door, he turned and said, "Hey, thanks, guys, for letting me help on this case with you. It means a lot. Now more than ever."

Higgins looked at Jackie, "What's he talking about?"

"I'll tell you all about it over coffee, boss," replied Jackie.

Billy left and decided to walk home, which wasn't that far, only a mile and a half down the road. As he strolled along, passing by the shops and offices, a slight mist filled the air, and looking at the edge of town; he saw a rainbow stretching across the horizon. Billy smiled and thought, *This is a good sign.*

Jackie got busy looking up the address of Jenny Lipton. Then she remembered that she had dialed Tom Lipton earlier and got his voice mail. Grabbing the phone, she checked to see if he had returned her call.

"Hi, Detective Summers, this is Tom Lipton returning your call. Please try again later."

Jackie dialed the number again.

"Hello, this is Tom."

"Hello, Mr. Lipton, this is Detective Jackie Summers of the Albany Police. I have been trying to locate your mother, Jenny Lipton. We are investigating a crime committed at the high school she attended some years ago and wanted to ask her some questions concerning some of her fellow students. Do you think she would be able to help us?"

"I don't know, Detective, my mother rarely talks about her high school days. From what I gathered from my grandparents, she didn't really have good memories there. She didn't have many friends, at least any she could confide in."

"I would still like to try to ask her some questions. It's very important that I speak with her."

"Well, I would like to be present when you meet with her."

"That would be fine," Jackie replied.

"I will meet you at the Hillside Apartments on Hillary Street at ten o'clock tomorrow morning. It's a sixty-five and older community."

"That would be fine, see you tomorrow morning. Bye."

Jackie hung up the phone and looked at Johnny and Higgins. "That went well. I am going to visit Mrs. Lipton tomorrow morning with her son. Let's see what dirty little secret Jenny is hiding."

There were clouds forming in the sky, and it looked like it would be a rainy evening today. Billy just walked into the house and smelled something cooking in the kitchen. "Is that my papa I hear coming in?" said the voice from the kitchen.

"I smell apple pie, is that my Melody baking my favorite pie. And where is Susan? I know you're hiding around here somewhere."

Susan jumped up from behind the couch. "Here I am, Grandpa."

At the same time, Melody came from the kitchen with oven mitts in her hands and gave Billy a big hug.

"Hello, Dad, how is the big case going? And how was Oregon? I hear it's a beautiful state. Lots of farms and big trees."

"Oregon turned out to be more beautiful than I thought, Melody. More beautiful than I thought. And I am glad you are here because there is something I wanted to talk to you about."

"Sure, Dad, what is it?"

"Well, you know how much I like to go on about the old days, my old friends at high school, the ball games, when I first became a firefighter, and the time I first met your mother."

"Sure, Dad, you told me how you first met and fell in love. I've heard many times."

"I loved your mother with all my heart, and I miss her every day. I can't describe how I wish she was still here. It's been five years since your mother went to be with the Lord, and now I need to ask her and you if I can start seeing a woman again."

"Dad, I think that would be great, and I think Mom would not want you to be alone. You are a good man and a great dad, and you deserve to have someone share life with you. But why now? Does it have anything to do with the Oregon trip?"

"As a matter of fact, it does. Do you remember when I once told you about my old high school sweetheart, Rose?"

"I do. I was about eighteen at the time. I was sitting on the back porch crying after Tony Blair broke up with me. You told me how you and Rose were going to get married someday, and then her father whisked her off to another state. Wait a minute, don't tell me she is the one you went to see in Oregon?"

"It turns out she had information about Clyde. Detective Summers wanted me to go along. Well, I guess the spark got lit all over again. Turns out, she is a widow and has a big two-hundred-acre farm, and well, we picked up where we left off. Seems she still had feelings for me that never went away. And you know something, Melody. I still have feelings for her. So I am asking. Is it okay with you?"

"Dad, you know that I want only for you to be happy. I know Mom is gone, and I miss her too. But she would want the same thing for you. Go for it."

Billy gave Melody a big hug. "Thanks, kiddo. And now, how about a piece of that apple pie with ice cream, chocolate syrup, jimmies, and whip cream."

Melody laughed as she headed into the kitchen. "Dad, you'll put yourself in the hospital eating all that. *No* chocolate syrup or jimmies. Maybe a little whip cream if you're good."

"Yes, mam. Just give me some of that apple pie." As he grabbed Susan up and carried her into the kitchen.

It was nearing two o'clock and almost time to head to the pub to see if Peter McCord was there. Jackie dialed Billy to let him know.

"Hello, this is Billy."

"Hi, Billy, it's Detective Summers, we are heading to the pub in a few minutes. Do you want to meet us there?"

"Will do, I'll get my jacket and meet out front."

Billy hung up and bolted out the door. It was raining, so he threw his jacket on and grabbed his baseball cap from the back seat, jumped in the car, and backed out of the driveway. Higgins, Jackie, and Johnny were already on the road heading toward the pub. Billy was only a few blocks from the pub when he saw a man walking on the sidewalk in the rain at a fast pace. Being the firefighter Good Samaritan he was, he pulled over to offer him a lift.

Rolling down the window, "Can I give you a lift, pal? You look like you're in a rush not to get wet. Where you headed?"

"To the pub down the street."

"I'm going there myself, hop in."

"Billy Sutter, glad to meet you."

"Peter McCord, thanks for the lift. It's nice to meet you too."
Billy just laughed.

"Must be that rainbow. I knew it was going to be a good day."

"What was that?"

"Oh nothing, just thinking out loud," replied Billy.

As Billy drove up to the pub, he could see a lot of cars already parked and older gentlemen walking in. He parked the car in the parking lot next to the pub, and they both got out and started walking in.

"I don't think I ever saw you come in here, Billy. Are you from around here?" asked Peter.

"Actually, I don't live far from here, I'm just not that much of a bar person. I am here to meet three detectives to interview someone."

"Really, do I know him?"

"Well, the person we are here to see is you, Peter," replied Billy.
They stopped, and Peter looked at Billy, surprised.

"What do the police want to talk to me about?"

"They just want to jog your memory from when you worked at the high school doing landscaping."

"Well, you could have warned me on the way over here, but I guess it's okay. I always want to help the law."

Billy could see Higgins, Jackie, and Johnny walking down the street toward the pub.

"There they are now, shall we go in? The first round is on me."

The rain let up some as they all met at the front entrance of the pub.

Higgins shook Billy's hand. "Hi, Billy. Who is your friend?"

"Everyone, this is Peter McCord."

They all looked surprised.

"I'll explain, let's go in before we all get drenched."

They entered, and Higgins found a table close to the door. They all sat, and Billy ordered the first round as the waitress came over to the table.

"I'll have a Bud Light, please." Peter ordered a Coors, Johnny, a Jack Daniel's on the rocks, Higgins ordered a Blue Moon, and Jackie ordered a margarita.

"Thank you, be right back with your drinks," replied the waitress.

"So, Billy, you didn't tell us that you already knew Mr. McCord here. It's a pleasure to meet you, sir," said Higgins.

"Well, we actually just met on the way here. I saw him walking in the rain and offered him a lift. It was coming down pretty hard," replied Billy.

"Well, I'm glad you stopped. Did Billy tell you why we wanted to talk to you, Mr. McCord?" asked Higgins.

"He did. It's something about my days a long time ago, working for the high school. I hope I can help."

"I hope so too. You may have read in the papers about the body that was found in the basement boiler room a few days ago. I know it's a while ago, sir, but do you, by chance, remember who built the two walls down there for the storage area?" asked Higgins.

In the meantime, the waitress returned with everyone's drinks.

"Here you go, Bud Light, Coors, Jack on the rocks, Blue Moon, and a margarita for the lady, enjoy!"

They all turned their attention back to Peter. Peter took his drink and tried to remember staring off past everyone sipping his beer.

"I know I used to go down there a lot to get supplies. I was still in my twenties at the time. You guys were just kids then. I may have even seen you there. Let me think. I believe it was in 1966 when they did that job. I'm trying to picture a face. I remember them working down there. That face, that face. He was a rugged type of guy. Big guy with a black beard, always wore a gangster hat, you know, the one turned to the side like a newsboy hat. I know he was older than me, probably by about fifteen years. He had a helper with him. It was a girl. It was a young girl. Maybe his daughter, I don't know. But they did the job on the weekend when there were no students around. It's been a long time. Let me think about it for a while. It should come back to me. It will probably come back when I'm thinking about something else."

Jackie and Johnny were both taking notes as Peter spoke.

"Well, it's something to go on," said Jackie.

"There has to be more in that yearbook. We are missing something," replied Billy.

They sat for a while longer, going over what they had so far, trying to put the puzzle together piece by piece. The jukebox was playing "Unchained Melody." Billy just looked up at Jackie.

"That was our song. Rose played it all the time. Funny, seeing her and now hearing that song. It feels like time has stood still."

"You will see her again, Billy. Be patient," replied Jackie.

The sound of men talking among themselves at the bar and the rain beating on the roof made for a quiet time sitting and drinking, passing the time and pondering their case.

Higgins turned to Johnny and said, "Kid, why don't you go back to the school tomorrow and see if you can dig up anything? Walk the grounds, go through the halls, check the gym, go back to the boiler room, and try to see if anything jumps out at you."

"Will do, boss."

"Jackie, you are heading out to visit Jenny Lipton tomorrow, correct?" asked Higgins.

"Yes. I will be meeting with her and her son at the Hillside Apartments on Hillary Street at ten o'clock tomorrow morning," replied Jackie.

Peter suddenly remembered, "Wait a minute, Lipton, Lipton, that's it. That's the guy who did the job. I remember now because every time I heard this guy's name, it reminded me of the tea company. You know, Lipton Tea?"

"Are you sure Peter that was the guy who built the wall in the basement?" asked Higgins.

"I'm sure of it. But you have to remember, he was a lot older than me. If he is still alive, he has to be in his late nineties. He may not remember the last time he farted. Oh, excuse me, Detective, I forgot there was a lady in the room."

"That's quite all right, Peter. I grew up with five brothers, and I work in an office with a bunch of men. I'm used to it," replied Jackie.

"But he's right," said Johnny. "Even if he is alive, he may not even remember doing the job in 1966."

"Well, I guess we'll find out tomorrow when I see Jenny if it was her father who did the job and if she was the helper. It seems kind of odd though, a young girl hauling large blocks around. She must have had arms like Rocky. I can't see anyone messing with her if you know what I mean."

Billy just sat there drinking his beer and listening to all the ideas being thrown around, trying to keep his mind on the case and trying to think of when he could see Rose again. Still, he felt something was missing, and it was in that yearbook. It was getting close to six o'clock, and everyone was tied. Higgins made the first move, finishing his beer, he said.

"I'm pooped. I'll see you all tomorrow at the office. I have to get some sleep."

"Good idea," said Billy. "Can I give you a lift home, Peter?"

"I think I'll stick around for one more. Thanks anyway."

"Okay then, I will see you all tomorrow morning. I want to take another look at that yearbook anyway," replied Billy finishing his drink.

Higgins reached over to Peter to shake his hand.

"Thank you, Peter, for all your help. We may put a dent in this case yet."

"You're welcome, Detective," replied Peter, raising his glass.

So leaving Peter alone with his drink, they started for the door and went home, for tomorrow would be a busy day.

It was three hours earlier in Oregon. Rose was in the kitchen preparing dinner, cutting celery and onion for a tuna salad, when the door opened, and Ron Jr. walked in. Coming up behind her, he gave her a big kiss on the cheek.

"Hi, Mom, need some help in here?"

"No, I'm fine. You do enough around here. You just park it, and let me worry about dinner."

"Okay, Mom, but first, I need to wash up and get this trail dust off me."

As Ron washed his hands at the sink, Rose turned to him, whipping her hands with a dish towel. She walked over to him while he washed his hands, both looking out the kitchen window at the vast farm with the cows and horses grazing in the field.

"Ron, how would you feel if I started dating a man?"

Ron stopped washing. His hands still under the water turned to his mother.

"Wow, I didn't see that coming. I guess I wouldn't mind. I mean, I want you to be happy, Mom. Have you met someone? Do I know him? Does he live here in town?"

Rose walked over to the bookshelf and pulled out her high school yearbook. She then brought it over to the kitchen table, where they both sat down, and she opened the page with Billy's picture and pointed to him. Ron looked at the picture and the inscription next to it. "I will always love you, Rose," signed Billy.

"Was he your?"

"Yes, Ron. Billy was my high school sweetheart. We would have been married if your grandfather hadn't gotten transferred here to Oregon. We lost touch after a while. I met your father. We ran this farm together. And then the Lord took him. A couple of days ago, a detective who came from New York asked me some questions concerning a case they are working on. It happened many years ago, but the detective brought Billy along. He is a retired firefighter who still lives in the old neighborhood and is helping them on the case. Well, seeing him, after all these years, we both still had feelings for each other. I would like your blessing to see him."

"Mom, you know I will always support you. I love you, and I want for to be happy. Sure, I know Dad is gone, but he wouldn't want you hanging around here on this big farm alone. I can handle things here. It's crazy, but like you always told me, 'It's all in the Lord's timing, not ours.' Go for it, Mom."

Ron looked down at the picture. "I got to admit, Mom, even then, you had good taste."

Rose gave Ron a pinch in the rib, "*Oh*, you."

After dinner, Rose and Ron sat outside on the back porch, watching the sun go down over the mountain.

"So, Mom, tell me about Billy. What's he like?"

"Oh, I think you would like him, Ron. When we were in high school, all he talked about was becoming a firefighter. And that's exactly what he did. He was liked by everyone at school. Played baseball and football and always watched out for the little guy. Billy always respected me and my friends. The teachers loved him. The only problem that Billy had was with Clyde Butcher. He was the school bully. Nobody liked him. He was always picking on kids smaller than him. Even the teachers didn't want him around. But he never bothered Billy because he knew Billy could kick his butt."

"What happened to this Clyde Butcher?"

"Well, that's why the detective and Billy came to visit me. They found Clyde's body behind a wall in the basement boiler room, tied to a chair dead. Seems he has been there since 1969. When he didn't show up at school anymore, everyone thought he moved or gone into the army. So they came to see if I remembered anything. I guess they are going around to as many of the old student body asking questions. Billy said they are even trying to find some of the old teachers. I hope they find what they are looking for."

"Wow, Mom, that's pretty amazing. If they hadn't found that body, you would have never connected with your old boyfriend. You know, Mom, it's funny how things work in this world. I'm with you, Mom, you deserve to be happy. We haven't had a vacation around here for some time, you know. The harvest is in. The ranch hands can handle things. Why don't we take a trip to New York? I hear the colors are beautiful in the trees this time of year." Ron smiled.

"You know. I didn't raise such a bad kid after all." She smiled, then Rose threw a dish towel at him.

Billy paced around the living room, going over the last couple of days in his mind. The pieces of the puzzle to the case were beginning to come together a little piece at a time. Peter McCord's statement shed some light on who built the wall in the school basement. But that was only part of it. The front section of the wall had to be closed in later on. One thing had nothing to do with the other. Even if Jenny's dad put up the side walls, it doesn't mean he killed Clyde and closed him up in there. There was still no proof. Something was still missing. This was going to take some time. Billy looked out the living room window at the school. Then he began thinking about Rose.

He let his mind wander back to the ranch walking up the dirt path with her holding hands, kissing her by the horse corral and the moonlight and the glow on her face and hair. It was then that his subconscious kicked in, and he remembered the time back when they were dating, sitting on the beach at night watching the waves roll in. There was a full moon that night also as he looked into her eyes just before kissing her. Her face and hair had the same glow, the same radiance that drew him to kiss her once again. Fate had given him a second chance, and he was going to take it. Billy sat down in his recliner, kicked up the leg rest, picked up the phone, and dialed. There was one ring, two rings, then, "Hello, Billy, I knew it was you."

"I was just thinking about the time we went to the beach and watched the waves beating up against the shoreline that moonlit night. Do you remember?" said Billy.

"I do remember that night. I remember the way we looked at each other. And the sound of the waves crashing up on the sand. The gulls riding the waves. The full moon. How could I forget? I was just sitting here in bed, reading a Hallmark book and thinking about the time we climbed up Bear Mountain. We went all the way to the top. I remember being able to see for miles around. We both felt like we were on top of the world."

"We were, Rose. I always felt on top of the world when I was around you."

"I told my son, Ron, about us. He wants to meet you. From what I told him about you, I think he likes you already. He mentioned taking a vacation in New York together. We haven't been away for some time with the farm and all. I would like to see the old neighborhood and the school, and you and I have some catching up to do."

"Indeed, we do. I will be your tour guide, milady."

"Why, thank you, sir, you're a true gentleman." Chuckled Rose. "How is the big case going?"

"Remember the guy who used to mow the lawn at school, Mr. McCord? We had a talk with him today, and he remembered that it was Jenny Lipton's dad who built the walls in the basement boiler room in 1966. But he never put a door on it. So we don't know who closed up the front section when Clyde was put in there. Seems like each time we interview someone, we get another small piece of the puzzle. The question is, how many pieces are we going to need to figure out who killed Clyde? I wish you were here with me to help. You were always good at figuring things out."

"Well, let me get things in order here, and I will let you know when Ron and I will be arriving. I'll bring my Sherlock Holmes hat."

They both laughed, holding the phone to their ear and enjoying the sound of each other's voices. Billy, with his legs up, watched the rain beating up against the living room window.

By morning, the rain had let up, and Jackie was on her way to see Jenny Lipton. She didn't know how this was going to go down with her son there. She was determined to find out what little secret she was holding on to about Clyde Butcher. As she drove on the freeway for the Hillary Street exit, Jackie went over in her head what questions she would ask and how she would ask them since this was a touchy issue with this woman. Jackie knew she had to use good police work here in case she had to come back on a second visit or third. She didn't want to scare Jenny off. She knew Jenny had information tucked inside her that could lead to a suspect, maybe even the killer.

She had to be gentle as a dove and wise as a serpent. Getting off the exit, the Hillside Apartments were just up the street. The rain started coming down a little harder now. She found a parking spot and jumped out; she ran to the main entrance and found the directory inside. Jackie began scanning to find Jenny's apartment number.

"Jenny Lipton, number 405. Okay, Jenny, let's see what you have bottled up that head of yours."

Jackie stepped into the elevator, and up she went. *Ding*, first floor; *Ding*, second floor; *Ding*, third floor; and *Ding*, fourth floor. The door opened, and there, right in front of her, was 405.

"Okay, Jackie, let's get this done."

She knocked, and within seconds, a voice from behind the door answered, "Yes, who is it?"

"My name is Detective Jackie Summers, Mrs. Lipton. I would like to ask you a few questions about a case we are working on concerning Clyde Butcher. May I come in?"

Jackie could hear Jenny unlocking the door, then the door opened, and to her surprise, a very attractive thin well-defined woman stood before her.

"Please come in, Detective, sit down. May I get you something to drink?"

"Water will be fine, thank you," replied Jackie.

Jenny returned soon with a glass of water, then sat down, cleared her throat, and looked directly at Jackie.

"My son couldn't make it here today. I know he wanted to be here, but he had other engagements. I read the newspapers about Clyde. You must have a lot of questions for me, and if you've been talking to any of the other students, they must have told you about Clyde and me. I know everyone thought Clyde and I had a thing going, but we didn't. That school had a thousand eyes. I didn't have to tell anyone anything. They all just figured something was going on. I wasn't that pretty like the other girls. I never had a boyfriend in school like a lot of them did. And I know all the girls there hated Clyde. None of them would ever go out him."

"Jenny, was Clyde forcing you to do something against your will? Was he threatening you with something you couldn't get out of?"

"It was during midterm testing. We were taking our math midterm exams. Clyde was sitting in the next aisle just behind the girl next to me. I always had a hard time in math class. My father said if I didn't pass with at least a B score, he would put me in the special needs class where the dumb kids go. I couldn't face any student there being in a class like that, it was just degrading. Anyway, I could see the girl next to me writing her answers down, so I peeked over and wrote down the correct answers. Well, Clyde spotted me, and when he got me alone in the hallway, he pulled me aside and said that he was going to the principal to tell him what I had done. Something like that would have gotten me expelled. I was scared and didn't know what to do. He said he wouldn't tell if I did what he asked. He took me down into the basement boiler room area to that storage room and made me get on my knees. I don't have to tell you what happened next. He made me do that twice a week for a year. He knew no girl would ever date him, so I guess he figured this was a way to make up for it. I knew some of the kids saw us sneaking off. I just let them believe what they wanted to believe. When I read the newspaper about what happened to him, I didn't know whether to laugh or cry. Laugh because that bastard got what he deserved, or cry because that was a horrible way to die. Either way, I was glad."

"Jenny, did your father ever find out about what Clyde was doing?"

"No, my father would have killed him if he ever found out. He probably would have killed me too."

"We were told that your father built the side walls to that storage room in the school basement, is that correct?"

"Yes, he did."

"Did he have any help on that job?" asked Jackie.

"Sometimes my older brother, Jimmy, would help him, but I don't know if anyone helped him on that job. I was still a junior at the time in the tenth grade."

"We met yesterday with the man who used to mow the lawn for the school back then. He told us that he remembered your father had some help. He said it was a girl," replied Jackie.

Jenny thought for a moment but couldn't remember her father ever using a girl to do block work.

"My father was very particular about his work, Detective. As far as he was concerned, doing block work was no place for a woman. He wanted to get in and get the job done and get out. He was fast, and he was good. The whole town knew his workmanship. He didn't mess around. Maybe your guy was mistaken. It was a long time ago."

"Jenny, is your brother Jimmy still alive?"

"Yes. He is in a Veteran's Home up in Albany. After he came home from the Vietnam War, he wasn't quite right. He spent some time in a POW camp with a lot of his comrades. He was tortured and saw many of his friends die there. Sometimes he has flashbacks and bad dreams. He was a kind and gentle soul when he went into the army in late 1966, actually just after my father finished that job at the school. But when he came out, he was a changed man. He would go into a rage if you looked at him the wrong way. He was very hot-tempered. My father couldn't deal with it. He told him to go find his own place if he couldn't control his temper. So he left. He found a place in Southern California with a few of his old army buddies. They all seemed to have the same problem. I can't tell you how many times my father had to go bail him out of jail. The years have calmed him down. Now he lives with guys like himself with counselors and small groups where they can talk about their problems. I think it's for the better. A least I know he is in a safe place with people who are taking care of him."

"Do you ever go to visit him?"

"I go to see him once in a while. He always said to me as I walked in, 'My baby sister, I will always watch out for you, I won't let anyone hurt you.' Funny, he was so strong back then, ready to defend me, now he can hardly take care of himself," replied Jenny with a tear.

"Well, Jenny, I think that's all the questions I have. You have been most helpful. Thank you."

"I'm glad you came here today, Detective. I have wanted to tell this to someone for over fifty years. I can now let it go. Thank you, Detective."

Jackie reached into her pocket and pulled out a card.

"This is my number. If you think of anything else or just want to talk, you can call me any time, any hour."

"Thank you again, Detective."

Jenny walked Jackie to the door and let her out. Jackie had many ideas going on in her head. Closing the elevator door, she watched as the floors went by, and when the doors opened, she bolted for her car to get back to the office and go over all her notes. This puzzle was beginning to take shape now.

In the meantime, Johnny was busy at the school, walking the halls and looking at pictures of past principals and teachers. There were many photos of baseball and football games with cheerleaders jumping in the background. Johnny found one photo of four football players standing in a group. Their names were under the photo: David Weston, Lewis Stanley, John Thompson, and James Lipton. Johnny took out his cell phone and took a picture of the photo with the names. As he walked a little further down the hall, he came to a glass cabinet with photos of students who served in the military. The photos went back to World War I. As he scanned through all the photos, he came upon a face he looked at in another photo, James Lipton. It was a boot camp photo taken before he went to Vietnam. Johnny took a picture of this photo also. As he walked on, he came to the cafeteria where there were a lot of photos of past students in goofy and playful themes, just fun photos. As he looked through all these, he spotted one photo of a group of hippies with long hair and beards, cut-off shorts, and holding up beers. The beach was in the background, and written by each name in pen was a name: Davey, Lewis, John, and Jimmy, and the date, 1966.

Something sparked in Johnny's head as he took a picture of this photo also. He continued inspecting different parts of the school for any other little tidbits of the school's past. Then he came to a door and opened it to see the football field. He scanned the field from the sidelines, from one end to the other, looking at the bleaches, and the fifty-yard line, trying to imagine it in 1966, visualizing the players on the field in their old football gear and the crowds cheering, the cheerleaders jumping up and down just like in the photos in the hall. Then suddenly, it hit him. He ran back to the hall, where all the photos were. Stopping at the first photo of the beach group, then he went over to the military case, looking at one photo, then to the game photos and the four players. He then went to the records room and asked for a copy of a yearbook from 1966. The clerk behind the counter went to a room where they kept many documents, records, and old yearbooks. She came out and handed one to Johnny.

"This is our only copy from that year. You will have to return it when you're through with it, officer."

"No problem, miss. I promise to bring it back, thank you," Johnny replied.

Walking quickly through the hall and out to his car, he started for the office to compare his findings. As he pulled out of the school parking lot, he noticed Billy just coming out of the house. He pulled over and rolled down the window.

"Hey, Billy, are you heading to the office?"

"Yes, I am, can I catch a ride with you?" he replied.

"Hop in."

Billy jumped in and noticed Johnny excited.

"What's up, Johnny? You look like you're ready to boil over with news of some kind," said Billy.

"I think I may have stumbled on to something new to the case. And it's a good thing I saw you because you could be a big help with what I have to show Higgins and Jackie when we get back to the office."

When they entered the office, Higgins and Jackie were sitting at Higgins's desk going over Jackie's interview with Jenny Lipton.

"Hey, Billy, hey, kid," said Higgins. "How did you make out at the school, kid?"

Johnny dropped the 1966 yearbook on Higgins's desk and pulled out his phone to show Higgins and the others the pictures he took in the school hallway.

"Jenny Lipton had a brother who went to the same school. He graduated in 1966. From the photos in the hallway, he went into the army right after graduating. He was also on the football team, and look at these two pictures. This one with him and four of his buddies, and this one of the same four on the beach. Notice anything about them?"

They all gazed intensely at the two pictures, then Billy spoke up, "Yes, they all have long hair, hippies. There were a lot of them when I went to that school also."

"Exactly," said Johnny. "I got to thinking about what Mr. McCord said about a girl helping Mr. Lipton with that block wall job at the school basement. Then I thought maybe it wasn't a girl. Maybe what Mr. McCord remembered seeing was Jenny's brother Jimmy with long hair."

Then Jackie remembered what Jenny said during their interview.

"He's right. Jenny told me that her brother sometimes helped his father with jobs. This must have been one of the last jobs he did with his dad before going into the army. He would then have to have his hair cut, of course."

"Kinda makes you wonder why he joined the army so quickly after graduating, doesn't it? Jackie, where is her brother now?" replied Higgins.

"He's in a Veteran's Home in Albany. Jenny told me he spent time in a POW camp in Nam. Saw a lot of buddies killed, was tortured. I don't know how much information we would get out of him now," replied Jackie.

As Billy looked over the pictures and thought about what Johnny and Jackie said, he said, "I have a feeling Jenny is not telling us everything about her brother, I mean."

"Johnny, get some hard copies of those pictures. I think I'll take another ride to see Richard Peterson," said Higgins. "In the meantime, why don't you two try to go see this Jimmy Lipton in that Veteran's home and see what you can get out of him if he remembers anything that is?"

Just then, Billy's phone rang; it was Rose.

"Hello."

"Hello, Billy, it's Rose. I just wanted to let you know that I have a plane ticket to New York, Albany Airport. I should arrive tomorrow evening at about six o'clock. Ron can't come. He has some horse-trading to do. Can you pick me up? I can't wait to see the old neighborhood again."

"Sure thing, Rose. I want you to meet my daughter Melody and my granddaughter Susan. They are excited about meeting you too," replied Billy.

"Great, I'll see you then. Bye."

Billy hung up and turned to Jackie, who was just sitting there with a big smile on her face.

"What?"

"I didn't say anything." She grinned.

"Don't you have some calls to make?"

Jackie smiled and then got on the computer to find the number to the Veteran's Home in Albany. Within a few minutes, she was dialing.

"This is the Albany Veteran's Home, Linda Jones speaking, how may I help you?"

"Hello, this is Detective Jackie Summers, I was wondering if you have a man there by the name of James Lipton?"

"One minute, and I'll check, please hold. Yes, will do."

"Would it be possible to see him today?"

"I'm sorry, Detective, but visiting hours are on the weekends from nine to three only. They are very strict about that. Can I make an appointment for you, Detective?"

"Yes, please, make it for ten o'clock this Saturday."

"All right, Detective, I have you down for Saturday, ten a.m."

"Thank you, Linda. Well, that's done."

Billy sat down next to Jackie, dazed. "Rose is coming in tomorrow evening. I'm picking her up at the airport. I am a bit nervous. It's been a while since I did this sort of thing."

"Don't worry, Billy. You'll be fine, an old Romeo like you. I think you should take her out to a nice restaurant tomorrow night, talk about old times, maybe walk down to the beach, go to the amusement park, and go on the Ferris wheel together. You can see a lot from up there. And then let nature take its course."

"Got it all figured out, do you?"

"Of course, I'm a woman. We always had it figured out."

Billy just rubbed his hand through his hair and smiled. At the same time, Johnny came back in with hard copies of the pictures he took at the school. He gave copies to Higgins, Jackie, and Billy. Five minutes later, Higgins got up from his desk and pulled Johnny by the sleeve.

"Come on, kid, let's pay Mr. Peterson another visit." And out the door, they went.

"He sure seems like he is in a rush," said Jackie.

"He seems like his wheels are always turning upstairs. He is on to something. Let's hope Mr. Peterson has some answers for him," answered Billy.

Higgins and Johnny pulled up to Richard Peterson's house and parked. They got out and walked up to the front door and knocked. Within a few seconds, the door opened, and out came the coach.

"Hello again, Detective. I gather you have more questions for me. I hope the case is going well."

"Thank you, Mr. Peterson. I have some photos here that I would like for you to look at for me."

Higgins handed the coach the three pictures from the school hallway. Examining all three, he looked up at Higgins and Johnny.

"This first one of the kids on the beach and this one of the four football players are the same kids. This one of the soldiers here is Jimmy Lipton. It's a shame what happened to that kid. A real shame."

"You mean about him being in a POW camp in Nam?"

"*No*, because of what happened one night in the summer of 1969. They were all friends out, driving around partying and drinking. Jimmy was driving the car when a produce truck coming around a corner collided with them and drove the car off a ledge on the side of the road. The car rolled about five times down the hill onto the rocks below, killing three of them. Jimmy found himself in the hospital with fractures and bruises. The other parents blamed him for the deaths of their sons. There was a trial, and the judge gave Jimmy a choice. Go to jail for ten years, or go into the army. Jimmy chose the army. It was a big thing around here, not like today when they just haul you off to jail. The law was a little more lenient then. They figured a few years in the army would straighten a kid out and give him more of a sense of responsibility. Sometimes it worked, sometimes it didn't. Anyway, no one knows what they were doing out there that night, and no one ever found out. It's still a mystery."

"How long was Jimmy in the hospital?" asked Higgins.

"*Oh*, I would say, if my memory serves me correctly, about ten days. I believe, five of the days, he was in a coma, and they didn't know if he would ever come out of it. But eventually, he did, then came the trial and then off to the army."

"Did you ever see his sister Jenny and him together with friends?" asked Johnny.

"I can't say that I actually ever saw them together, but there were the school dances, we had a lot of them. Most of the students were there, and there were always teachers around watching. I imagine Jimmy was there to watch his sister. He was always pretty protective of her, being the big brother and all. I was a little protective of my little sister too. It's what big brothers do, I guess. He had his own set of friends, and she had hers."

"I wonder if we could get the old medical records to find out what Jimmy's alcohol level was," said Johnny to Higgins.

"It will be pretty tough getting records that far back, but who knows, kid, we may get lucky. Mr. Peterson, thank you again for your time, I hope we won't have to bother you again."

"Not at all, Detective, anytime."

"Let's take a ride over to the hospital, kid, to see if you're hunch pans out."

Higgins and Johnny strolled out through the picket fence and hopped in the car, and Higgins got on the phone to Jackie. Jackie's phone rang a couple of times before she picked up.

"This is Detective Summers."

"It's Higgins, how did you make out with the Veteran's Home, Jackie?"

"We have an appointment for ten o'clock this Saturday morning. They only have visitation on the weekends."

"Damn, okay, is Billy going with you?"

"Me, Billy, and Rose."

"Rose? How did she get involved in this?"

"She is coming into town tomorrow to visit Billy. She was there at the time, Higgins, maybe her presence there would get Jimmy to talk to us. She may even jog his memory if he's not all drugged up."

"Okay, but you ask the questions. You know what they say about too many head cooks in the kitchen. It can get messy."

"We'll keep it together, boss."

"Good, Peterson gave us some good info on Jenny's brother, Jimmy. Right now, we are headed to the hospital to check out some records. I'll fill you in when we get back to the office."

"You got it, boss."

Billy stood by the window, looking out and holding a cup of coffee while Jackie was speaking to Higgins. After hanging up, she walked over to him, put her hand on his shoulder, and gave him a little shoulder rub.

"You're like a nervous sixteen-year-old going on his first date. Relax, Billy. Obviously, you both have been thinking about each other for over fifty years, and it's only right that fate brings you both together again. Don't worry, you'll be fine."

"I guess I am a bit nervous. A lot has happened in the past few days with the case, Rose, seeing people I haven't seen in fifty years. I get the feeling that something is going to screw it up, and at this time in my life, I don't want anything to go fowl, if you know what I mean."

"I guess we've all been there, Billy. But after getting to know you these past few days, if Rose doesn't scoop you up, I may just ask you out, Romeo."

Billy relaxed, and they both laughed, standing there, gazing out at the cars going by and the city life.

Melody was busy in the kitchen putting the finishing touches on the strawberry shortcake with Susan. The clock was ticking, and Billy hadn't come down yet to head to the airport. Cleaning her hands on her apron, she went to the bottom of the stairs and called up to him.

"Dad, are you ready? The plane will be landing in forty minutes, you'll be late. Dad"

"Almost done, be right down."

As she turned to go back into the kitchen, she heard footsteps coming down the stairs. She turned to look up and see Billy dressed in one of his beautiful gray suits. His black shoes shined like mirrors, a new black tie and hair combed like a movie star.

"Wow, how did Clark Gable get in this house?" Melody said with a great big smile. As Billy came into the kitchen, Susan jumped up off the chair and ran over to Billy,

"Grandpa, Grandpa, you look like you're going to a wedding, wow."

Billy looked at Melody and blushed, raising his eyebrows.

Melody straightened Billy's tie, brushed off his suit with her hand, and guided him toward the door.

"You get going now. We'll be here when you get back. Dad, you'll be fine. *Go.*"

Billy gave Melody a kiss, then bent down and kissed Susan, checked himself one last time in the foyer mirror, then opened the door, and walked out to the car that he had detailed the night before. Melody and Susan watched as he backed out of the driveway and headed toward the airport to pick up Rose.

The airport was about ten miles away, and on a Thursday evening, there wasn't too much traffic. The night was clear and cool. It was the perfect evening for a nice outside café dinner with the perfect companion. Driving up to the entrance of the airport, Billy followed the signs to the pickup area along a two-lane road. Off to his side, he could see planes landing and taking off. As he approached the pickup area, he scanned the terminal platform for any sign of Rose. Passing by taxi cabs and vans and Uber cars, he noticed just up ahead Billy spotted a bright red flowing dress blowing in the wind, a wide-brimmed straw hat, long silver hair streaming down from behind, and a fancy brown carry bag. As he came closer, he could see that smile staring at him as if she knew him coming from afar. Billy pulled alongside, got out, walked confidently around the car, took her in his arms, and kissed her. All fear was gone once he saw her.

"You look beautiful, Rose. I thought I was gazing at an angel as I drove up and saw you."

"Thank you, Billy. And you look dashing in that suit."

"Your chariot awaits, milady."

Billy took Rose's suitcase and put it in the trunk of the car, then came around and opened the passenger door for her as all gentlemen should. Then buzzing around, he got in, looked at Rose as if he could not believe she was sitting right beside him, took a deep breath, and off they went exiting the airport and into town.

As they passed by buildings and diners, Rose just gazed at the past. Billy turned a corner, and Sam's old bakery was still there. There was a younger person behind the counter, but old display cabinets with fresh baked donuts and buns were still inside.

"Oh my gosh, Sam's bakery is still here?" asked Rose.

"Yeah, Sam passed away some years ago, but the kids and grandkids run the business now. Still the same, everything from scratch just the way Sam did it," replied Billy.

"Remember when donuts were only four cents, and the pies were five dollars?" asked Rose as she put her hand on Billy's shoulder.

"How can I forget? You used to drag me there every Friday night for some of Sam's donuts, especially those apple cider donuts. And Rose, they still have them." Smiled Billy.

"Oh my gosh, Billy, we have to go there. I have to have some of those apple cider donuts."

"*Okay*, how about this Friday night?"

She looked at him the way she did fifty years ago. "It's a date."

Further on down the road, they passed by their old Lutheran Church. They put in a new parking lot and remodeled the outside of the building. Just up ahead, Rose spotted a very nice French café with tables outside, umbrellas, and waiters with long white aprons serving people wine.

"That's new. I always wanted to go to a French Café."

"I'm glad to hear that because that's where we are going. I made reservations for us."

Rose's eyes widen with joy and excitement. Her hand went from Billy's shoulder to his hand resting on his shift stick. He just looked at her with that Humphrey Bogart face. "Here's looking at you, kid."

As they walked into the main entrance, a young girl approached and greeted them and, in a French accent, asked, "Welcome, do you have reservations?"

"Yes, two please for Sutter," replied Billy.

"*Ah*, here we are. I have your table right over here, please follow me."

They followed the girl outside to a table over by a grapevine and a trellis overhead with low hanging lights, wine glasses on the table, and a fountain just to their left with angels and flowers pouring water. There was French music playing softly throughout the restaurant, and people, speaking to each other in low tones, enjoyed the beautiful evening.

Billy pulled Rose's chair out for her like a gentleman, then sat across from her to see her face.

"Your waiter will be here momentarily, enjoy your dinner," said the girl.

Rose looked all around. From where she sat, she could see a good portion of downtown and the park across the street where they played as kids with the swings and slide. She felt like she was in a bubble somewhere in time, looking at her past. But she knew it was real, looking at Billy, sitting right across from her. She put her hand on Billy's. "Thank you, Billy."

Billy just smiled and held her hand in his as to never let go, when suddenly, their waiter arrived with a bottle of red wine and a towel hanging over his arm.

And in his French accent and said, "Good evening, my name is Claude. I will be your waiter this evening. Would you like to try our house red wine before I take your order?"

"We would indeed, thank you," replied Billy.

Claude rested the bottle on his toweled arm and poured a glass for Rose, then Billy. Rose watched as Billy took the glass, rolled the wine around gently, then smelled the edge of the glass and tasted the wine as a true wine coinsure. Rose smiled and took a sip, then gave Billy the look of approval.

"We'll take a bottle of this fine wine, Claude," said Billy.

"Yes, sir, and would you like to order now, or do you need a minute?"

"Give us a minute, thank you," replied Billy.

Billy and Rose picked up their menus and browsed through them while sipping their wine when Billy saw something that looked good. Soon Claude returned to take their order.

"Have you decided?"

"Can I ask what is the Soupe à l'oignon?"

"Ah yes, this is a traditional French soup made of onions and beef stock, served with croutons and melted cheese on top," replied Claude.

Rose looked at Billy and said, "That sounds very good, being a farm girl, I like beef and cheese."

"Okay, Claude, make it two, thank you," said Billy.

"Yes, sir, may I take your menus?"

Claude left, leaving Billy and Rose to the beautiful night ahead of them. Rose just leaned back with the glass of wine in her hand and inhaled the air of her old neighborhood, gazed at Billy sitting there in front of her, a bit older perhaps, but it was her Billy, and she knew she was his Rose.

"Do you still live in that same house across the street from the school?"

"I do, I know it's crazy, but once I got on the fire department, I knew I was here to stay, and when my parents died, I couldn't sell the place. It was where my roots were. It's where I grew up. Melody and Susan love the place, and when I go, it will be theirs."

"I'll bet you're a great father and grandfather. I can just see you bringing them down to the firehouse and letting them ride the fire engine and climb up the ladders."

"Yes, I've done that many times with Melody when she was a little girl and with Susan. We like to go bird-watching together in the park. She loves birds and listening to them sing their songs to each other. She likes to capture them on film with her camera. She's making a scrapbook with all the birds she took pictures of so far. She's a tiger, that one," said Billy.

"I wonder what it would have been like for us if we had been able to do the things we planned to do back then," asked Rose.

"At the time, I guess it just wasn't meant to be. Now, is the time, Rose?"

Billy placed both his hands on Rose's as he said these words to her. As he leaned forward to kiss her, Claude showed up with their dinner. They both smiled and sat back as Claude placed their plates in front of them."

"Be very careful, the plates are hot. Bon appétit."

"Well, Melody and Susan sound wonderful. I can't wait to meet them," said Rose.

"And they can't wait to meet you." Billy smiled as he tried the soup. "Wow, that is hot." The two laughed and sipped their wine while the music played "As Time Goes By."

It was nine o'clock now, and Billy took his time driving home to let Rose take in as much of the old neighborhood as she could, even though it was dark.

"Are you sure it's okay staying at your place? It won't be awkward with Melody and Susan?" asked Rose.

"We have an extra bedroom upstairs next to Melody's room that we rarely use. We all discussed it. It'll be fine. And besides, I make killer pancakes like my dad used to make. Firehouse style."

"Well, let no one say that I ever turned down Billy Sutter's firehouse killer pancakes."

Billy pulled into the driveway and could see that the lights were still on the inside. He stepped out and around the car to open Rose's door. As she stepped out, the first thing they saw was the high school across the street. She just stood there looking at the old school where she met so many friends and had so many good times. Then her eyes caught sight of the entrance to the basement just off the side of the building.

She turned to Billy and asked, "Is that where they found Clyde?"
"Yes, it is," he answered.
She got chills just thinking about it as she stared at the doorway.
"Shall we go in? I imagine the girls up and waiting to meet you."
Billy took Rose's arm, and they walked up to the front door. Just as he was about to open it, the door opened, and Melody greeted them.

"I saw you pull in the driveway, Dad. This must be Rose. It's so nice to meet you, please come in. And you too, Dad." She chuckled.

"Very funny, ha ha," he mused as he stepped in.

Susan was standing behind Melody in anticipation of meeting Rose.

"And this must be Susan I've heard so much about. Your grandfather tells me you like bird-watching? There are plenty of birds to see on the farm, plus some wild animals roaming around the hills will come down and show themselves, like mountain lions, black bears, and bobcats," said Rose.

"Oh, wow, I could fill an entire scrapbook with pictures of all kinds of animals and birds," Susan replied.

"You'll have to talk to your mother and grandfather first, Susan," said Rose.

"Why don't we go into the living room and sit down, you must be tired from that plane flight? I made some coffee and cheesecake," said Melody.

"That sounds wonderful, Melody. I am a bit tired from that five-hour flight," replied Rose.

The smell of fresh coffee coming from the kitchen was like heaven for Rose. Coffee made from New York water was a treat she hadn't had since she left years ago. Just the feeling of being back brought back memories of her school days with her girlfriends having pajama parties and talking about boyfriends and hairstyles and clothes. She lived a farm life for so long, hardly going anywhere. Farming was a tough life; getting up early to run a farm, and farm animals took up most of the day. When she did vacation, it was close to home within driving distance. A lot of things could go wrong on a farm: droughts, sick animals, and flooding were just a few to mention.

Billy sat across from Rose, just watching her soak up all the memories while she drank her coffee. She gazed around the room, looking at all Billy's honors, certificates, and medals over the fireplace and around the room on the walls. There were pictures of him when he first became a firefighter, pictures of him and his wife, and Melody as a child from a baby to college graduation. Next to Melody's pictures were pictures of Susan from baby to present. She could see Billy's whole life on his walls, and it was a good life. One she wanted to be a part of. The night was going well as they sat chatting and getting to know one another; Billy's cell phone rang just as he was about to grab another piece of cheesecake. It was Johnny. He had found some old newspaper articles in the archives of the school about the accident involving Jimmy Lipton. He had photos and Jimmy's statement to the police after he came out of his coma in the hospital. Johnny told Billy that Higgins wanted everyone at the office early tomorrow to look them over.

Billy hung up the phone then looked at Rose and asked, "Want to take a ride to the police station with me tomorrow and meet the rest of the crew? It may be an interesting day."

"I'd love to meet them. Although I must say, Billy, going from firefighter to detective, you do get around," Rose laughingly replied.

"Well, my mother always did say that I had ants in my pants. I'm not one to sit around watching TV. I have to be doing something productive if you know what I mean."

"I do indeed, Billy," replied Rose, "you haven't changed a bit. You were the same way in high school. You always had to be on a team. I guess I'm pretty much the same way, especially after running a farm for over fifty years. My husband and I were always up at the crack of dawn, ready to take on the day, and it didn't end until we went to bed. Although, I never had a chance to do any detective work before. This could prove to be a new avenue for me, maybe I can help."

Melody just sat back and watched as Billy and Rose remembered so much about each other. Each remembering some little quirk or saying that each one did or said. But it was getting late, and one by one, they all began yawning.

"Come on, Rose, let me show you your room, you must be exhausted," said Melody.

Melody grabbed Rose's bag and led the way down the hall to a spare bedroom. As she followed Melody, Rose turned to Billy and gave him a wink. It was the same wink she gave him back in high school, signifying, "I'll see you tomorrow."

Billy had a sudden flashback of her entering her front door when she was eighteen, giving him that same wink. He had to pinch himself to make sure he wasn't dreaming as he kept his eyes on Rose walking down the hall. Susan followed close by her mother, carrying Rose's small bag. Billy got up and turned out the light, then went upstairs to bed, feeling his age creeping up as he climbed the stairs.

All eyes were on Billy and Rose as they walked through the door into the office. Billy first led her over to Higgins's desk.

"Rose, I'd like you to meet Detective Gerald Higgins, the lead detective on this case. And this young buck over here is Officer Johnny Wallace, a new recruit working the case with us. And I believe you know Detective Summers, sitting over there. Everyone, this is Rose. I guess by now, Jackie has told you two gentlemen our entire history. Rose and I go way back. We went to high school together and were much more in those days. Rose remembers a lot of the students also and some of the goings on that accrued during 1969."

"Do you still keep in touch with any of your old high school girlfriends, Rose?" asked Higgins.

"Only a couple of them now and then. We will call each other every few years or so to see how each other is doing. I believe the last time we saw each other was at my husband's funeral. But we didn't really talk about our school days. All I could think about was losing Ron. They were just there to comfort me."

"I see. I'm sorry for your loss, Rose," replied Higgins.

"Thank you, Detective."

"Johnny said he found some old articles on Jimmy Lipton's accident back in '69," asked Billy.

"He did, Billy. We have them spread out over there on the table. Photos and everything." Higgins pointed to the table.

Billy and Rose walked to the table and picked up one of the articles. Billy began reading as Rose looked at the photos. Rose had to look away, seeing a photo of three body bags lying on the ground next to a mangled car. Another photo showed Jimmy Lipton lying on his back in an ambulance being treated by a paramedic, all bruised and bleeding. He had an oxygen mask on and looked to be unconscious. A third photo was of all four of them with football uniforms on only a few months before the accident. Meanwhile, Billy sat on the edge of the desk, reading the article.

"According to Jimmy's statement, they were driving back from football practice to drop one of the guys off home when a truck came around the corner and hit them head-on. Cars didn't have seatbelts back then, and Jimmy went flying through the windshield and rolled down the hill on some grassy area. It's amazing he didn't get killed. The others weren't so lucky. They were trapped in the car, and the force of the truck hitting that vehicle just pulverized them. They died instantly. It says here after he came out of the coma and learned about his friends being killed, he went a little crazy. I guess they were all pretty close. It says he didn't remember anything else that happened that night."

Then Rose remembered the four students as she looked at the photo of them with their football uniforms on.

"I remember them. They were always hanging out together. The school called them the four horsemen. Because when they played against another team, we always won when they were playing. If one guy was out and couldn't play, we always lost the game. They were invincible together on the football field. One of my girlfriends liked one of them. So I always got the scoop on who was playing. I remember she was all broken up when she found out he got killed. They canceled all the games for the next two months after the accident. Without the four horsemen, we could never win a game."

As Rose looked, once again, at the photo of Jimmy lying in the ambulance, she noticed something strange hanging from Jimmy's pants.

"This is odd," she said, holding the photo and showing it to Billy and the rest in the room. "See this hanging from his pants. It's a black rabbit's foot. Clyde used to wear one just like it. He had it hanging on his pants just like Jimmy in this photo. Clyde always had it with him. I never saw anyone else with a black rabbit's foot at school except Clyde. It was like his trademark. It's funny seeing Jimmy with the same thing."

"That is odd. I wonder if there's a connection between the two. Two hot shots at the same school trying to impress whoever they can impress. One with a fancy black leather jacket and hairdo. The other is a jock on the football team. Maybe they both figured they got all the luck they can get. Or maybe they belonged to some secret society where the rule was all members had to wear a black rabbit's foot like the Free Masons," replied Higgins.

Jackie jumped in on this scenario as she tapped her desk with the pen.

"Why would a football jock need a rabbit's foot anyway. He's got all the girls falling all over him already. They are winning all games as long as the four horsemen are all playing, that is. The only one that I can see who needs a rabbit's foot is Clyde."

Johnny chimed in, leaning up against the other side of Jackie's desk.

"She's got a point there. Jocks don't need any luck to get what they want. They all have their own little following, whether they be bodybuilders, fighters, or ball players. It is kind of odd to see Jimmy wearing a rabbit's foot. But it's a good thing Rose noticed it. I didn't catch it when I looked at that photo."

"Good job, Rose. This could be a lead in the case, even if it is a fifty-year-old one. Billy, you have one heck of a woman there. I'm glad you brought her in today. You're one heck of a woman too, Jackie. Tomorrow, you have to go to the Veteran's Home to see Jimmy. See if you can jog his memory a bit about that rabbit's foot. Shake him up a bit. He may know something about this Clyde fellow that meets the eye. Maybe there was some rivalry between them going on. He may be the connection between what happened to Clyde and that accident. After all, three people lost their lives. Clyde wasn't the only victim at that school in 1969," said Higgins.

"I think I'm going to like being a detective. And I like my partner. Just like old times again, Billy," said Rose with a smile.

"Just like old times." Smiled Billy.

The others just looked on with that thought in mind, *Here we go.*

It was obvious Billy and Rose had hit it off and were starting on a new journey together, a little older and a little wiser.

The next morning was foggy and damp as Jackie and Rose pulled up to the Veteran's Home to pay Jimmy a visit. Both women had this strange feeling that Jimmy knew something about Clyde's death and had been holding some secret within for the past fifty years. But what? They exited the car and walked up the steps into the foyer where the main offices were. Seeing a door that said the administration, they knocked and heard a voice say, "Yes, come in." Jackie opened the door to see a middle-aged man sitting behind his desk dressed in an army reserve uniform with a nameplate on the front of the desk, "Captain John Dean."

"Yes, may I help you?"

Jackie stepped forward and showed her detectives badge and said, "Captain Dean, I am Detective Jackie Summers, and this is Rose Masters. You have a man here by the name of James Lipton, I believe. We would like to have a few words with him concerning an old case that has just reopened."

"I think that can be arranged, Detective. You are aware that some of our patients here are on some form of drug to help with any disorders they may have. Sometimes these drugs can block out any long-term memories these men and women have to prevent flashbacks of war experiences so that they don't become harmful to themselves and others. Let me call in one of the orderlies to take you to him."

Captain picked up the phone and dialed the second-floor desk. "Would you send an orderly down here to bring some people up to see Jimmy, please? Thank you. Someone is on their way down to show you to Jimmy's room, Detective," said the captain.

"Thank you, sir," replied Jackie.

Rose just stood back and remained quiet, looking around the office and out the window at the other patients walking the grounds, some with the help of aids pushing them in wheelchairs. *What a place to spend the rest of your days*, she thought to herself as she stared out the window. *And what would Jimmy, who was now in his seventies, be like? Would he be pumped up on drugs and remember what he had for dinner the night before?* Only time would tell when they got to his room. Soon an orderly walked in to escort the women to Jimmy's room.

"This is Corporal Jones, ladies, he will escort you to see Jimmy," said the captain.

The corporal directed the women to follow him. They walked down a long hallway with pictures of military officers on the walls and cabinets of Medals of Honor donated by the families of those who had died there, along with their photos. Then coming to an elevator, they stepped in and went to the second floor. There wasn't much said between them as the orderly brought them to room 24 and gave two knocks on the door. As he stepped in, he said, "Jimmy, there are some ladies here to see you. Okay for them to come in?"

"Yes, corporal, I'll see them."

Jackie and Rose stepped in to see Jimmy sitting by the window, staring out, holding a cup of coffee in his left hand and an unlit cigar in the other. From the side, Rose noticed a scar that ran down his left arm and also one on the left side of his neck. His hair was gray with a few black streaks. Jimmy turned, looking at the two women. His eyes fixed on Rose with a bewildered look.

"Do I know you?"

Rose stepped forward and sat down on the bed, keeping her eyes set on Jimmy while Jackie scanned the room, looking for anything familiar that would help the case. Then Rose took hold of Jimmy's hand. He just looked down, then back at her.

"Jimmy, I don't know if you remember me, but we went to the high school here together back in 1969. My name is Rose Palazzo."

Jimmy turned away and looked back out the window when Rose mentioned the high school with a scared look on his face. Rose turned at looked at Jackie who also noticed it. Jackie just walked slowly around the room while Rose talked to Jimmy. She went over to his dresser, where there were pictures and personal things scattered on top, including a high school yearbook from 1969. Jackie looked carefully at all the objects moving them around with her finger very quietly so as not to let Jimmy see what she was doing. They both knew he must be drugged up, so he would hardly notice anything they did. Behind the small lamp laying on the dresser was a picture. Jackie picked it up and saw that it was the same picture that Johnny had shown them of the four football players standing on the football field, "The Four Horsemen." There was also a picture of Jimmy just out of boot camp in his army uniform. And as she picked up the picture to examine it, her eye caught the black rabbit's foot just behind the picture. She picked it up and held it in her hand, wondering why he had kept this all these years.

Rose then asked Jimmy, "Jimmy, do you remember any of your high school years or students and friends you hung out with in those days? We are investigating the murder of a student who attended the high school you went to. We know you graduated in 1966, but your sister Jenny attended the school during the years 1967 to 1969. We also learned that you were very protective of your sister, that's a good thing. Do you remember a student by the name of Clyde Butcher?"

Jimmy turned and looked at Rose. His face changed to a look as if he were going into battle.

Then he turned again, gazing off out the window, and replied, "I remember him. Tough guy. At least he thought he was. Always a bully, always bothering some kid smaller than he was. Always bothering the girls, trying to pick up on them, and them wanting nothing to do with him because he was a freaking jerk. I remember my buddies always wanted to go put a beating on him to teach him a lesson. I told them to leave him alone, that someday day some kid smaller than him would do the job for us. That's usually what happens to bullies. They just need a taste of their own medicine by a guy smaller than a bunch of jocks who can kick his ass. All I know is one day, he was gone. No one knows what happened to him. It was about the same day that my buddies and I were in a car accident. I lost three of my best friends that night. We were all drinking. I found myself in the hospital for ten days, five of those days in a coma. Well, there was a trial because I was driving. The judge offered me to jail or the army. I chose the army, went to Nam, and spent some time in a POW camp, saw my army buddies killed. I guess I just lost it after that. Didn't want anything to do with the outside world anymore. There is nothing out there I want. I have friends here now. I'm happy here. My sister Jenny comes to see me once in a while too. You mentioned Clyde, what about him?"

"It was Clyde who was murdered, Jimmy. Some construction workers found his body a few weeks ago in the basement of the high school behind a block wall in the boiler room. The wall your father built for a storage area. Do you remember it?" asked Rose.

"Yes, I do. My friends and I used to help my dad with large projects sometimes. This was a small one, so I helped him build the wall down there. But the school didn't put a door on it. They just wanted it for storage."

Then Jackie came over to Jimmy and asked, "Jimmy, you said your friends used to help your dad also doing block work?"

"Yes, we all knew how to build block walls. My dad was a good teacher. Plus, it gave us a chance to make some extra cash. My friends weren't afraid of hard work," replied Jimmy.

Then Jackie showed Jimmy the rabbit's foot.

"Do you remember where you got this rabbit's foot from?"

Jimmy took the rabbit's foot from Jackie and held it tightly in his hand.

"I do, my friend Davey Weston gave it to me the night of the accident. I've had it ever since. I keep it to remember them by."

Then Jackie asked, "Were you with them the whole night of the accident, Jimmy?"

"No, I had some things my dad wanted me to do around the house first. Then they came and picked me up by the football field around nine o'clock. We went and had some drinks at the bar, and it was shortly after that we had the accident, and they were killed. I still feel responsible for their deaths. I should never have drank that night."

Then Rose took Jimmy's hand.

"What's done is done, Jimmy. Things happen. You can't let it eat at you. They will always still be your friends."

Jimmy gave Rose a little smile. Jackie scanned the room once again, noticing a drawing on the wall by Jimmy's bed. It was a picture of *The Man in the Iron Mask* sitting in his cell in chains. She went over to take a closer look. It was a color drawing about eight by nine inches, and at the lower right-hand corner were initials. It looked like DW, a date, 1966.

She turned to Jimmy and asked, "Jimmy, who did this drawing? It is very good."

"Oh, Davey drew that when we were in high school. He did it in class one day, doodling with a highlighter. Davey loved reading all the classic novels. *The Man in the Iron Mask* was his favorite one.

He said that's what he felt like sitting in math class. He was a great artist."

"Mind if I take a picture of it, Jimmy?" asked Jackie.

"Not at all," he replied.

Jackie then took out her cell phone and took a couple of pictures of the drawing, including a close-up of the initials and date on the drawing.

Just then, Corporal Jones stepped in.

"Sorry, ladies, but it's time for Jimmy's treatment. I'm afraid you'll have to leave now. Ready, Jimmy?"

"Yes, corporal, let's get this over with. Nice to meet you, ladies. Please come again. I'm always up for company. We don't get many visitors here, you know, and if you see Jenny, tell her to come more often."

"I'm sure you, ladies, can find your way out," said the corporal.

Jimmy got up and followed the corporal out the door and down the hall. Rose and Jackie followed behind to the elevator and watched as they disappeared around the corner. The elevator door opened. They got in and just looked at each other.

"Well, that was interesting, to say the least," said Rose.

"Indeed, it was. But I believe he gave us a lot of information. At least his memory is still good. We may have to pay him another visit," replied Jackie.

As they stepped out of the elevator and walked toward the car, Rose turned to look up at the window of Jimmy's room. Jimmy was looking right back at her. She gave him a smile and waved goodbye. He, in turn, waved back and smiled. She didn't take her eyes off him as she got into the car. Then Jackie backed out of the parking spot and off they drove back to the office. As they drove back to the office, Jackie couldn't help but wonder why Dave Weston gave Jimmy that rabbit's foot.

"Didn't it strike you strange about that rabbit's foot, Rose? I keep thinking about what Johnny said back at the office, you know, how jocks don't need a rabbit's foot. They pretty much can have whatever they want, and back then, as it is today, it was girls," asked Jackie.

"It does sound a little strange now that you mentioned it. And Jimmy also said that his friends wanted to put a beating on Clyde, but he stopped them. Makes you wonder what those other three were doing before they picked up Jimmy to go drinking, doesn't it? I don't know about you, but my wheels are spinning. Let's run this by the guys when we get back to the office. You know, Jackie. I like this detective work," as she gave Jackie a big smile and replied Rose.

It wasn't long before they arrived at the office. Higgins, Billy, and Johnny were at their desk, going over their notes and digging for more information on the computer. As Jackie and Rose walked in, Billy was staring at Rose with a big smile, that same smile he had when they were dating. She knew he couldn't wait for her to get back. And she couldn't wait either. They both gave that "Honey-I'm-home look." The others noticed it too.

"So how did it go with Jimmy?" asked Higgins.

"Well, it looks like some of the pieces to this puzzle are starting to come together. Jimmy still has the rabbit's foot. He said that Dave Westin gave it to him the night of the accident when his friends were killed," said Jackie.

"That was also around the time Clyde disappeared, isn't it?" asked Billy.

Then Rose chimed in, "Jimmy told us that he and his friends used to help his dad do building block jobs for extra cash. And Jimmy said that he was the one who helped his dad build the wall down in the basement of the high school. And he also mentioned that they never put a door on it, which means someone else sealed up entrance to that room."

"Good thinking, Rose. Looks like we're getting closer to this solving this case. You are all doing a great job. I don't know where we would be if it weren't for Billy, Rose, and of course, you, Johnny. I never had a better bunch of partners in my life. Why we may even find out who really killed Kennedy." Laughed Higgins.

"I'm thinking about what Rose just said, guys. What were Jimmy's friends doing before they picked him up that night of the accident? There is something missing here, and the sad thing is, the only ones that know the answer to that are all dead," said Jackie.

"Johnny, I want you to find out if any of the parents, siblings, cousins, or anybody who is still alive and around at that time can be questioned. Someone has to remember something of what happened that night besides that accident. Any little piece of information will help. Find out if there were any dances that night and who was there. Something tells me that this rabbit's foot could hold the key to solving this whole case," said Higgins.

"Well, I don't know about you, guys, but I am going to take this beautiful woman to dinner, and we are not going to talk about this case the rest of the night," said Billy as he went over to Rose and put his arms around her and gave her a kiss right on the lips, then turning to the others, smiling and said nothing but took Rose's hand and led her right out of the office and to his car and off they went.

And with that, Jackie started for the door.

"Where are you going?" asked Higgins.

"I am going home, taking a good hot bath, getting into my pajamas, curling up with a good book on my couch, and going to sleep, and for the next twelve hours, not think one thought about Clyde Butcher. Good night, gentlemen."

Jackie strolled out the door without even looking back. Higgins and Johnny just looked at each other.

"You know that sounds like a good idea. Think I'll go home, take a nice hot shower, watch the game, and hit the hay myself," said Johnny as he shut down his computer and walked out the door.

Higgins found himself alone in the office, looked around, jumped up, and said out loud, "What the heck am I doing here? I could use a shower myself. A nice glass of whiskey and some pleasant dreams too. Good night, office, see you in the morning." He then got up, shut down his computer, and marched out of the office whistling "My Wild Irish Rose."

Billy and Rose strolled down the street toward the restaurant, arm and arm. A cool breeze was blowing down through the buildings, giving Rose a chill as she held Billy's arm close to her. It was like old times again. Rose couldn't believe she was here walking down the street with her first love, holding onto him as if to never let go. It was a dream that she didn't want to wake up to. As they got closer to the restaurant, Rose looked at the name above the door, "Eddie's Place."

"You've got to be kidding me, Eddie's Place, he's still here?" said Rose.

"Well, Eddie died a few years ago. His kids run the place now, but the food is still the same. Nothing has changed. I thought you would like to come here. We have a lot of memories here, Rose. The place is still the same inside too. All the pictures on the walls of the stars that have eaten here, like Dean Martin, Frank Sinatra, Sammy Davis, Joey Bishop, and the whole Rat Pack ate here."

Rose held Billy closer as they entered the restaurant. A young girl greeted them holding menus, "Table for two, right this way, please."

Billy and Rose followed the girl over to a romantic corner table dimly lit with a candle. There was Italian music playing overhead softly as they seated themselves next to each other the way they used to.

The girl placed two menus on the table and asked, "Would you like to try some of our house wines made here?"

"Two glasses of your Rose wine, please," replied Billy.

"Yes, sir, I'll be right back with those."

Rose just looked all around at the pictures on the walls, the old ceiling fans, and the same tile floor. It was like stepping back in time. Their time. Billy just sat back and watched Rose take it all in, looking at her the way he did fifty years ago. No, nothing had changed, not even them. The girl soon came back with their wine and gently placed it on the table.

"Have you decided what you would like to order?"

They both looked at the girl and said together, "Lasagna," which is what they always ordered fifty years ago. Eddie's was the place to go for Lasagna. The whole town knew that. And the freshly baked bread that came with it. Billy raised his glass to toast. And as they both gazed in each other's eyes, Billy said, "Here's to our good old times we had together and the good times to come." As both glasses clang together, they both drank to their future. It wasn't long after that the young girl placed two dishes of Lasagna in front of them, piping hot with a basket of fresh baked Italian bread and a side of sauce for dipping the bread. Rose pulled her camera from her purse and took a picture of it.

"I have to send a picture of this to Ron to show him what he's missing in Oregon."

They both laughed, then grabbed their fork to dig in. It was the perfect night for both of them.

Higgins was sound asleep when the phone rang, causing him to jump out of bed and stumble around, looking for where the sound was coming from. He finally grabbed the receiver while looking at the clock to see what time it was, seven o'clock. "Hello."

"Higgins, it's Pete Fargo. We've been doing some forensics on Clyde Butcher's clothing. We found human hair on his jacket and pants. It is three different types of hair besides his own. Probably the people responsible for putting him behind that wall due to a scuffle. He must have put up a fight before they got him into that chair and tied up. I'll be here all day today if you want to come and have a look yourself."

"Okay, Pete, thanks, I'll be down later on today."

Higgins looked over at the bathroom door, scratching his head, knowing that he had to get in there and shave and shower. Scuffling over in his floppy slippers, he went and closed the door behind him and yelled out, "Good morning, Vietnam."

There was the smell of fresh brewed coffee and pancakes at the Sutter home this fine morning. Melody was at the oven flipping pancakes and listening to her favorite Bible study Chuck Swindoll, while Susan finished the last bite of her pancakes and got ready for school. The sound of footsteps came into the kitchen from the hallway; it was Rose, bright-eyed and bushy tail full of energy.

"You're up early, Rose. How about some coffee and pancakes? My own recipe," said Melody.

"You have to be up early on a farm, and I would love some coffee, Melody, thank you."

"How do you like being back in the old neighborhood roaming the streets with Dad?" asked Melody.

"Some places have changed, and some places haven't. It's still the same old neighborhood. Many of the old homes and parks are still here. But walking the streets with Billy makes me feel as if I had never left. Your father still has the same sense of loyalty and responsibility he had when we were back in high school. Always ready to protect the weaker guy and do the right thing," said Rose.

Melody turned from the stove and looked at Rose.

"He has always been a good father and taught us those qualities that it's not always about us but those who are in need. No matter who they are, rich or poor, it's nice to know that there is always someone there who is willing to help. Even the Bible tells us to help those in need. And in this house, the Lord comes first," replied Melody.

Susan just looked at Rose and smiled as she brought her dish to the sink and placed it in with the rest of the dirty dishes, then picked up her backpack and started for the door.

"The school bus will be here soon, Mom, I have to get going. Bye, Rose."

"Bye, sweetheart, love you," replied Melody.

"You have a great kid there," said Rose.

"She's like her grandfather in every way. Last month, there was a little girl being bullied by a bigger girl in the schoolyard, and Susan got right in between them and faced off with this bigger girl, and the girl backed down. From what I understand from the principal, she doesn't bother anyone anymore," replied Melody.

"That's just what Billy did to Clyde fifty-two years ago. Only Clyde didn't stop his bullying. But apparently, someone stopped him. I wish it could have been some other way, like the army or even some time in prison might have changed him. But to die the way he did? To be walled up alive? Nobody deserves that kind of death, not even Clyde. I have been mulling this over and over in my mind about who could have done it. I keep trying to picture all the students I knew back then in high school, and I can't think of anyone with that sick of a mind who could have done it," said Rose.

"Maybe it was someone not from the school. It could have been anyone in town or from another town. It may have been someone from his previous town where he lived who finally caught up to him and made it look like it was someone from here by putting him in the basement of the high school. This is not an easy case to figure out. You guys have your hands full on this one," said Melody as she sat down with her coffee.

As the girls drank their coffee, Billy strolled in.

"Is that coffee I smell?" As he walked over and kissed Melody on the forehead and Rose on the lips.

"We were just discussing the case, Dad."

"Yeah, this bugger had me tossing and turning all night. I had faces and places and old teachers and old fights going through my head like an old movie."

"Sounds like you and Rose had the same type of night. Give it time, Dad. I know between the detectives and Rose and you, you, guys, will figure it out," replied Melody.

Billy placed his hand on Melody's shoulder and gave her a fatherly rub.

"Thank you, Melody."

Rose had a puzzled look on her face as she sipped her coffee.

"What's up, Rose, you look as if you just went into a different world there for a second. Is it about Clyde?" asked Billy.

"Not exactly, Billy. I was just thinking about Jimmy Lipton. The guy Jackie and I went to see at the Veteran's Home. You know, Jenny's brother. I just keep thinking he isn't telling us everything. I know it was a long time ago and that he's had it pretty rough ever since his three friends died in that accident. I get the feeling he knows more of what happened that night and maybe just forgot or isn't saying. Call it a woman's intuition."

"Well, never let be said that I ever argued with woman's intuition. Let's take a ride down to the office and talk to Higgins and the others. See what they say," replied Billy.

"That sounds like a good idea, perhaps Higgins can get Jimmy on the phone to have an open conversation, so we all can hear."

"Let's go find out, Rose."

Melody couldn't help but laugh. "Boy, a firefighter turned detective, and a rancher turned detective. I guess you could call this a God-wink case."

"Well, Billy knows how to find that still burning cinder laying below the hiding in a building or that small child cramped down the closet in a burning home, waiting for someone to come find them. And me? I can weed out any groundhog hiding in the garden or wolf getting too close to the chicken house," replied Rose.

They all laughed as they finished their coffee. And Rose and Billy got up to get ready to head to the office. Melody picked up the cups and put them in the dishwasher, then went about her chores before she went to work herself.

Back at headquarters, Higgins was sitting behind his desk, staring at the pictures of teachers and students from old photos Johnny had gotten from the high school principal that he collected over the years. He was hoping Billy and Rose would come in to see if any of the photos would spark their memory. Time was moving on, and the captain was getting impatient about getting some kind of results. The clock just struck eight, and Jackie and Johnny came walking in with Starbucks in hand, ready for what was next.

"I'm glad you two are here. Any sign of Billy and Rose?"

"They just pulled up behind us. They should be in here in a second," replied Jackie.

Billy and Rose walked just as Jackie said, and Rose, with her northwestern accent, gave a nice "Good morning, everyone."

Everyone answered back with a good morning. As Rose moved closer to Higgins's desk, she noticed all the old photos.

"My gosh, Higgins, where did you get all these old photos?" she asked.

"Johnny was able to get them from the principal over at the high school. He had been holding on to them for a while. Some are left over from the principal that was there when you two went there. I was hoping maybe between the two of you, you might see something that could tie some links together in this case. There has to be something here we are just not seeing," said Higgins.

As Billy and Rose started looking over the photos, all kinds of memories began to flow through their minds, memories of dances, football games, and classes with their old teachers. Rose picked up a photo of her old history teacher, Mrs. Sonn.

"Wow, look, Billy, Mrs. Sonn. She was a great history teacher. I loved sitting in her class. I think all students there loved her."

"I remember my friend Henry Billings had a crush on her. Well, she was a good-looking woman back then. I wonder if she's still alive."

"Well, if she is, she's well into her nineties. I don't think Henry would still have a crush on her now," replied Rose.

The others just sat back and watched as these two scanned over the photos of their yesteryear, going back in time to the place where they first met and fell in love. It was like watching a movie. As Rose picked up some photos from under neat the pile, she happened on one of Jimmy and his friends.

"Look, Billy. It's a picture of Jimmy Lipton and his friends. The ones who died in the accident."

Higgins and the others came over to the desk to look at the photo. It was a large photo nine by eleven and still in good condition. It showed all four of them in front of Jimmy's car in the school parking lot sitting on the front hood. From left to right were David Weston, Lewis Stanley, Jimmy Lipton, and John Thompson. David Weston had a shoulder bag hanging off his left shoulder. And there was something written on the front that looked like initials. Jackie came next to Rose.

"Can I take a look at that, Rose? Johnny, will you pass me my magnifier on my desk, please?"

Johnny came over with the magnifier and handed it to Jackie. Looking very closely at the carry bag and at the initials, she noticed that it was the same initials on the drawing in Jimmy Lipton's room.

"What is it, Jackie?" asked Higgins.

"I saw this same initial on a drawing that David Weston drew for Jimmy in his room at the Veteran's Home."

Then Billy picked up the yearbook to look for David Weston's picture. Under each photo, the students always wrote some remark about the future. After flipping through the pages, he came upon David Weston's school picture. Under it read, to be a writer and artist, always keep track of what goes on in my life. Billy showed it to the others. As they all thought and wondered until Johnny stepped up and said, "It can only mean one thing. He kept a diary. I'll bet you anything, that's what's in that bag he's holding."

"The kid's right, that has to be it. I'll bet if we had that diary, it could tell us a lot," said Higgins.

"Do you think his parents would still have it?" asked Rose.

"I believe his parents are dead. They both died within a year of each other's a few years back. I believe the estate went to one of David's brothers. We could go check it out. I did some research on the three friends at home," replied Johnny.

"Okay, kid, you and I are going to take a ride to see David's brother. Rose, Billy, you guys have been a great help in this case. Jackie, see if you can't get hold of that captain at the Veteran's Home and get Jimmy on the phone. Perhaps you can pull some more out of him about this dairy if, in fact, there was a diary. Billy and Rose, why don't the two of you keep going through those old photos. Who knows, you may find some more links to this mystery in your walk down memory lane."

Higgins and Johnny headed for the door to check out the Weston residence and this supposed diary. Jackie made for the phone to contact the Veteran's Home, and Billy and Rose enjoyed every moment looking at the old photos from their school days.

Higgins and Johnny pulled up in front of the Weston home, an old colonial with a wraparound wooden porch and a front door with stained glass that dated back to the early thirties. The front yard was all manicured with roses lining the sidewalk. They opened the white wooden gate and started for the door. Higgins gave two knocks, and soon an elderly gentleman opened the door and greeted them. He seemed to be about in his late sixties with salt and pepper hair and a small mustache, and he had on a pastor's collar to indicate that he was a man of God.

"Yes, may I help you?"

"Pastor Weston?"

"Yes."

"Sorry to bother you, Pastor. My name is Detective Gerald Higgins, and this is Officer John Wallace. I suppose you've read the papers about the body they found in the basement of the high school?"

"Yes, I did read all about that. The papers said he'd been there since the late sixties. Is that right?"

"It is, sir. May we come in and talk, it won't take but a minute or so?"

"Yes, please come in."

They all went into the living room and sat down on a couch that must have been as old as the house. There were pictures of family all around them on shelves and mantels. One particular picture that caught Higgins's eye was of David and his brother when was around fourteen years old. The two boys were in front of an old fort, probably a vacation picture. David had that same shoulder bag hanging over his left shoulder.

"So, Detective, what is it I can help you today."

"Well, Pastor, it's about your brother David here."

"David?"

"Yes, did you ever know of David having a diary?"

"Why, yes, he didn't go anywhere without it. He always liked to keep a journal of the events in his life. It's a shame his life was cut so short to ever complete it."

"We believe there could be something in David's diary that may help us discover who killed Clyde Butcher. Your brother must have taken note of everything that happened during his school years. Things he couldn't tell anyone about but that he could write down and keep safe to himself. Pastor, do you have any idea what became of David's diary?"

"I was still a young kid at the time. When David was killed in the accident, my parents were so distraught with grief. When the police came to the house to bring back David's things they found at the accident, they refused it. They said they couldn't look at those things and constantly be reminded that their son was gone. I believe they just turned it over to evidence, and it must still sit somewhere on a shelf at the evidence building. I've driven past it a few times. It's a huge building. They must have evidence in there going back to the twenties."

"Yes, sir, I'm familiar with it. I've been in there many times. And yes, they do have stuff in there going back to the twenties. But you have been a big help to us, Pastor, sorry to bother you so early, sir."

"No bother, Detective, I was happy to. I hope you find my brother's diary, and it helps you to solve this case. And if it's all right with you, once you've finished with it, I would love to have it back home here where it belongs."

"I'll see that it finds its way home, Pastor."

They shook hands, and Higgins and Johnny followed the pastor to the door.

"You, gentlemen, have a blessed day."

"Thank you again, Pastor."

They headed back to the car, and once behind the wheel, Higgins turned to Johnny.

"We need to get into that evidence building and find that dairy. I don't know, but I have a hunch, it's just a hunch, but it might pan out."

Higgins started the car, and off they went to the evidence building uptown. The drive took a good forty minutes to get there. It was a huge building, seven stories high, and must have been two hundred feet wide and a thousand feet long. There was a guard at the entrance with three armed guards at the gate.

"Holy cow, this place is like Fort Knox," said Johnny.

"You know it, kid. They have stuff in here that would make your hair stand on end. Guns, drugs, cars, tanks, money, lots of money, and anything used as evidence are here. So we have to mind our Ps and Qs here. Do whatever they say. You got it, kid?"

"Yes, sir."

They pulled up to the gate and were greeted by the first guard. Higgins rolled down the window.

"ID, please." Higgins and Johnny both handed the guard their IDs. The guard scanned them and then said, "Wait here while I run these through the system."

He went into the guard building to put the info in the computer while the other two guards kept their eyes fixed on the car. Soon the guard returned with their IDs and handed them back.

"Okay, go through the gate here and follow it up to the main entrance, park in space marked P, that's your spot for the time you're here. Go through the main doors and see the guard at the front desk. You'll have to leave all weapons at the front desk before going in."

"Thank you, officer," replied Higgins.

As he started the car, they slowly drove up the driveway to the parking spot marked P and parked. They both got out and walked up the stairway to two big automatic doors that opened as they neared the building. Once inside, they saw a huge front desk with two guards sitting behind it. Higgins and Johnny walked up to the first guard.

"My name is Detective Gerald Higgins, and this is Officer Johnny Wallace. We are doing the investigation of a murder of a high school student that happened some fifty years ago. You may have read about it in the papers?"

"Oh yeah, that bully that the construction workers found in the high school basement."

"That's the one. We believe that there may be some information in a diary that belonged to one of the students that were killed in a car accident just around the same time the bully disappeared. Is there anyone here that can help us locate this one student's personal items?" replied Higgins.

"Do you have a name?" asked the guard.

"David Weston, and I believe the accident occurred in the summer of 1969."

The guard put the information in the computer and, in two minutes, came up with a bin number.

"You're in luck, Detective. There is only one name in the system for David Weston. And yes, we do have his personal items still here. I'll have to have an officer go with you while you and the other officer are in the evidence area. You will have to leave your weapons here. There are tables there to place the boxes on to view any items. Nothing leaves the building. Once you have examined the items, place them back in the box, and the officer accompanying you will place them back on the shelf. Understood?"

"Understood," replied Higgins.

Higgins and Johnny removed their weapons and handed them to the guard. In a few moments, an officer came in from a door just behind the front desk to greet them.

"My name is Officer Jim Cameron, I'll be escorting you into the evidence area. Please follow me. Have you been told the rules upon entering?"

"Yes, we have."

"Okay then, let's go in."

Higgins and Johnny followed the officer back through the door he came in from. They walked down a long hallway to an elevator and stopped. The officer pushed a code on the keypad, and the elevator doors opened. They stepped in, and doors closed behind them. They went down to a floor that was marked subfloor on the elevator pad. When the doors opened, their eyes widened to a room that must have had a thirty-foot ceiling with rows and rows and rows of shelves with thousands of boxes. The officer looked at them and then stepped out.

"Follow me, gentleman."

They exited the elevator and followed the officer down one of the aisles, passing by guns, huge plastic-wrapped bundles of money, and boxes that all had names and dates on them. They finally came to an area at the end of the aisle. The officer looked at the paperwork in his hand, then scanned the boxes in that area until he spotted a box on the shelf up high on the upper level. He went and got a rolling ladder and pushed it over to climb up and retrieve the box. Pulling off, he carried the box down and handed it to Johnny. Then the officer walked them over to a table where they could examine what was inside.

"I'll be just over here, Detective. Let me know when you are finished so I can put the box back."

"Thank you, officer."

Higgins and Johnny just looked at each other.

"Well, kid, let's see what's inside."

Higgins found the corner of the box and peeled back the edge slowly and opened it. They both looked in to find some clothes, a baseball hat, a wallet, and a comb that every boy carried with him in the sixties. Higgins reached in and pulled out the clothes and the hat. As he moved the clothes away, there, under it all, was the dairy. Next to it were some pens and pencils. Higgins reached in and gently took the dairy out. It was a beautiful brown leather-bound diary with a leather strap that wrapped around it. Printed on the front in gold lettering was the initial's DW. The dairy was still in pristine condition. Higgins gently untied the strap and opened the diary to read its contents. David wrote about one of the girls he had a crush on, on one of the pages. There was another entry about the football game they had just won, and one of the players broke his wrist, catching the ball to make a touchdown.

"I guess we should go to the last entry. The one just before the accident," said Johnny.

"Good point, kid."

Higgins gently turned each page until he reached the last entry:

June 17, 1969

Tonight, me and the guys, aside from Jimmy, decided to teach Clyde Butcher a lesson. We found out through a mutual friend what Clyde was doing to Jimmy's sister Jenny. The whole school is sick and tired of his bullying. And so are we. The teachers can't do anything to control him. He ruins the games when he is there in the stands, acting like an idiot, bothering the girls, and getting into fights with the guys. We tricked him into meeting us at the school basement to drink beer. He fell for it. After we got him drunk, he passed out, and we tied him to a chair in the storeroom we helped Jimmy's dad build. We tied his hands and feet and wrapped duct tape around his mouth. Then while he was passed out in the chair, we decide to block up the doorway and enclose Clyde behind it. We got the idea from an old movie, *The Canterville Ghost*, where the father walled up his own son alive for cowardice. We waited till he woke up to see one block left out so we could see in. When he realized what was happening, he was startled, trying to yell and scream. We told him that he was getting what was coming to him. That he would never bully anybody ever again, and this was his tomb. We then put the last block in place as he tried to yell and scream. What he didn't know was that we were going back later to let him out. To let him know that we don't want bullies in our school or our neighborhood, and we'll do anything to get rid of bullying from our town. Heading to pick up Jimmy now and go down to the beach to drink and party. I'm going to give Jimmy Clyde's black rabbit's foot as a gift. Let Clyde sweat a while behind that wall. Maybe he will change his ways, maybe he won't. Either way, this bastard is getting what he deserves. Jimmy will never know. Better he doesn't.

DW

"Holy cow, kid. So that's what happened. These three guys tried to teach Clyde a lesson, and it backfired on them. They were going to go back and let him out. Only thing is, they never got a chance to. Who knew they would all be killed that same night, all except Jimmy, that is. Talk about divine justice," said Higgins.

"What do we do now?" replied Johnny.

"Well, we have to take new evidence to the captain. He, in turn, has to present to a judge, and the judge will probably close the case since there isn't anyone to arrest. The suspects are all dead, and the victim. I guess we should call the officer back here to see what we need to do to get this dairy back to headquarters."

Higgins called the officer back and explained the situation. The officer, in turn, went over to the phone and called upstairs to see what procedure they needed to obtain the dairy. He came back and told Higgins that another officer would be down with all the proper paperwork to take the dairy. They waited a few minutes, and soon another arrived with all the paperwork, which Higgins signed and gave back to the officer, who, in turn, went into a nearby room to make copies. He soon came back, gave Higgins his copies then picked up the diary and handed it to Higgins.

"Is that it?"

"Yes, that's it, Detective, I'll guide you and Officer Wallace back to the main entrance if you would follow me, please."

Higgins and Johnny followed the officer back to the elevator and up to the main front desk, where the guard gave them back their weapons, and they headed back to the car. Pulling out of the parking spot, Higgins drove slowly down to the main gate where the guard checked the paperwork, then opened the gate, and out Higgins and Johnny drove back on to the main road for headquarters.

That day, Higgins, Jackie, Johnny, Billy, and Rose all sat in the captain's office as he read the dairy and David Weston's confession of what happened the night of the accident and the fate of Clyde Butcher. They looked up at Higgins, running his hand through his hair.

"Well, this is truly amazing. You all did a great job on this case. I'll present this to the DA, and he will probably just hand it to a judge who will finally close it. And rest in peace to those three guys who were killed. As for Clyde Butcher, God only knows where he is. Johnny, I am going to recommend you to be assigned to Higgins's team to become a detective. You did a great job, son."

As they all got up and went back into their office, they all plopped down at their desk with a sense of completion.

"So Billy and Rose, what are your plans now?" asked Higgins.

"Well, I think I would like to try my hand at ranch life in Oregon. I've been in this neighborhood too long. I think it's time for a change with someone who can teach me the country life." He smiled as he gave Rose a big kiss.

A few months later, under a beautiful flowered canopy on a lush green lawn on the Oregon ranch, stood Billy and Rose while the pastor read from the Bible, and Billy and Rose took their wedding vows. Seated up front were Higgins, Jackie, Johnny, Melody, and Susan, with Rose's whole family to witness the joining of two lovers who never lost that spark for each other.

Johnny would go on to become a fine detective, solving many cases on the Higgins team. Jackie became a lead detective in the homicide squad and would have her own team.

The dairy was returned to David Weston's brother, its contents never revealed.

As for the Four Horsemen, they remained local football heroes on the school wall of fame. And as for Clyde Butcher, his memory faded away like an echo. As if he never ever existed. Divine justice.

THE END

ABOUT THE AUTHOR

Tom Puma is a retired electrician and real estate agent. He has been writing since 1980. His first book, entitled The Adventures of Tom and Fiore, was published in 1982. Living like Tom Sawyer and Huckleberry Finn on Staten Island, Tom decided to write about their adventures as kids. Tom always believed in finding his true passion, which is writing, and tries to instill this concept in everyone he meets, finding that passion that lies deep within us. Tom lives in Cave Creek, Arizona, on his two and a half acres of property. When Tom is not writing, he enjoys studying history, Bible study, art shows, yard sales, singing Doo-Wop, and listening to opera.